CAPT. CRUNCH

GEORGE ONSTOT

FOR RUDY MAXAS
EVERYWHERE:

MAY YOU PASS QUICKLY AND
ACCURATELY

CHAPTER 1

Rudy Maxa turned off the ignition of his Volkswagen Passat and looked at the sunbaked parcel of land everyone called Burned Out Park. It had tall trees providing adequate shade, and benches and a playground—even a water fountain that, he had been told, dispensed cold, moderately clean H20. Still, it was a vision of tan and brown, the victim of a California drought.

Rudy jumped out of his car and pulled out the duffel bad containing the things he would need for the next hour or so: A regulation NFL football, a spare tire and a length of rope to tie the tire to a tree.

He looked around, checking things out. The only other creature he saw was the occasional squirrel. He had come here for the past several days, with only himself for company and conversation. Hot summer, new state, no friends yet. *Way to go, Mom.*

After securing the rope to one of the trees so that it dangled at chest height, Rudy grabbed the football and trotted backwards ten yards. Then he reared back, Joe Montana style, and fired a pass that missed the tire by a dozen feet.

He shook his head and muttered something nasty.

He hated being out here all alone, and he really hated missing a target he had nailed a hundred times before. Plus, he had nobody to run over and retrieve his poor throws. He needed to be his own slave out here in the heat, and that sucked.

His passes went through the tire about half the time. He threw the football again and again, and when he was successful, he felt lucky. Soon he felt so thirsty that he needed to get his water bottle. Rudy enjoyed water most when he was really thirsty, just as his meals always tasted best when he was famished.

Once hydrated, he stood under a tree and wiped the sweat from his face. Aside from the trees, the only shade in Burned Out Park came from a bronze statue of a horse. Rudy didn't know the significance of the horse and wasn't interested in it enough to read the plaque at its base. But there it was. Rudy didn't want to practice any more, so naturally he resumed it and started going at it twice as hard. He would push himself out here even if it was twenty below and his limbs were becoming frostbitten. Nobody got into the NFL by quitting practice the moment he got tired or thirsty.

Rudy took off around the park, running as fast as he could, over and over. He was no doctor, but even he knew that whenever he taxed himself physically to the limit, his brain released natural painkillers called endorphins that produced an intense high. He had spent many hours pushing himself hard enough to get some very long, enjoyable endorphin trips. But he wasn't here to get high; he was here to throw passes and continue his education as a quarterback. He kept at it, throwing his football at the tire from greater distances and a variety of angles. For him, there was something priceless about seeing his own pass sail thirty or forty yards and end up hitting his target. He could do that for the rest of his life without ever getting tired of it.

Sneering against the oppressive heat, he stepped back and threw his longest pass of the day. A decent spiral, it sailed over the bronze horse and kept going. Just then he saw someone appear, a figure who ran for the airborne football, snapped it up before it reached the hard, dry brown grass, and ran it back to Rudy.

"Nice pick, dude," the quarterback said, unable to see the runner clearly and assuming he was Rudy's own age. But then he saw that the smiling guy was a *man*, easily in his fifties, but tall and muscular and agile. "You look like you've played this game before."

"Could be I have," he said, still holding the ball. "I'm gonna throw long."

Rudy nodded and ran hard. He looked over his shoulder and saw that the man still had the ball.

"Keep going!"

"Where? Nevada?"

The man threw the ball. Rudy would have sworn that Dan Marino had tossed it—a beautiful spiral that threatened to stay up there forever. The boy ran and ran; as the ball came down, the receiver reached up, feeling pigskin on his fingertips…

But then all he had in his hands was dry turf, and the ball bounced away. Rudy lay there for a moment or two, wishing he could start sucking air back into his lungs and start feeling human again, when he heard cackling and felt himself being lifted back onto his feet.

"You'll never get into the Hall of Fame if that's

the best you can do." The man had righted him as if he were a rag doll and now stood face to face, a broad smile on his weathered face.

"What's your name?" Rudy asked him. "What should I call you? My name's Rudy."

"Call me Mitch. Heads!" Mitch punted the ball; Rudy watched it rise into the deep blue sky as if it would touch the sun.

"Mine!" Rudy settled under the ball, determined to show his older guy that he could make this simple catch after failing to pull down that long pass. Rudy, a born competitor, loved having someone he could show off for.

The ball came down, faster, faster, and he pulled it in. Then he went down.

He lay flat on his back, wondering what had happened to him, and at first he thought that a truck had hit him. But no; he looked up and saw Mitch standing over him, hand extended to pull him back up for some more.

"That hurt," Rudy said, trying hard not to vomit.

"If it don't hurt a little bit, it ain't no fun," retorted Mitch. He stepped away, picked up the ball and said, "Come and get it!"

Rudy got up, thinking, *This old guy is way too weird. But if he wants me to tackle him, why not? I'm half his age. I'll try not to hurt him.*

Although he wished neither to hit nor be hit, he caught up with the running man and grabbed his hips, taking him down just the way he'd been taught since his first day in organized football.

As the two tumbled to the ground, Rudy thought, *I sure hope I didn't hurt the old fart.*

But Mitch lay there laughing. "That's how to do it!

Didn't think you had it in you!"

Rudy took the ball away and said, "Now it's your turn! Go deep!"

To his amazement, he watched the old guy roll over, get to his feet and race across the dry, crunchy natural turf. Mitch weaved this way and that, faking out imaginary opponents, then looked in the quarterback's direction.

Rudy, so entertained by the spectacle of the old man's childlike showing off, forgot for a moment that he held the football and was expected to throw it. When he did, his pass went much too far.

"Oops," he muttered as he watched the ball fly over the bronze horse. But Mitch followed it and made a shoelace catch. Then he did a little victory dance, pumping his free hand and wiggling his butt.

Rudy knew that, in football, when his passing game worked, he needed to keep passing till it stopped working. So he sent Mitch on one pattern after another. Since arriving in California from Indiana, he'd had only his mother and himself for companionship and conversation. So he resisted the urge to ask Mitch certain questions—like why was a guy his age hanging out in deserted parks and horsing around with a teenaged boy like Rudy Maxa.

"Last one for today! Make it count!" Mitch, holding the football, motioned for Rudy to run. Then the big man reared back and fired a bullet that zoomed straight through the boy's arms and right out of Burned Out Park.

BAM!

Rudy had heard the sound of shattering glass enough times to know exactly where to find his football. He and Mitch dashed over to the parking lot and found the football in the backseat of someone's Buick, covered with shards of glass. Most of the window was gone.

"Busted," Rudy said as he reached in to retrieve his football. "Gonna cost some money to replace—"

He looked up just in time to see Mitch sprint off down the street like a little kid running home to Mommy and Daddy after misbehaving.

Thanks very much, Mitch. Hope I never see you again. But I have a feeling I will, and if I do, I hope you bring your checkbook.

CHAPTER 2

Rudy Maxa had a dozen reasons to be ambivalent about moving two thousand miles and several states west. But one good thing was that he'd be attending Claymore High, a school with a great football program. His parents had recently divorced and his mother, eager to resume her journalism career, had procured a position at the Claymore, California, *Transcript*. From their home in Terre Haute, Indiana, she had gone online and said, "Here's who I am, and here's what I can do." She knew that people in journalism quit, retired, died or got fired surprisingly often. Salaries were usually abysmal, the hours long, the work thankless. Graduates of America's premier journalism schools, who wanted to be superstars, refused to accept humble reporting jobs in third-rate markets. But to Kathleen Maxa, the *Transcript* gig looked acceptable.

"It's California, Rudy!" she'd shouted. "How many kids get to move to the Golden State? Plus, you'll be going to Claymore High. I'm sure you'll make their team, and who knows what could happen then?"

Mom Maxa also felt gratified that northern California was so far from her ex-husband in

Hoosierland. When they divorced, she felt he was being difficult for no good reason—he'd wanted sole custody of Rudy and tried to bribe the boy with a Volkswagen Passat. The kid accepted the car but moved to California anyway, infuriating Dad.

Rudy sat in the Passat near his new high school. He fully agreed with the zillionaire Malcolm Forbes, who'd had said, "Money is a nice thing to have." Rudy felt that way about his car. Not absolutely, positively necessary by any means, but a very rad thing to have just the same.

It's California! his mother had said more than once. Well, Claymore *was* in California—but very much northern and inland, so it wasn't any kind babes-and-beaches paradise from Hollywood movies. Without much effort, Rudy could look around his new home and convince himself that he was still in Terre Haute, Indiana.

As he stayed put in the car, he looked around and asked himself why so many jocks were out there suited up for football. The lady in the athletics office had told him that nothing would be happening till eleven o'clock—so how come there was *a lot* going on at just after ten?

He got out of his VW, put up its roof, locked its doors and hurried over to where the action was. The field seemed so full of guys too busy to answer his questions, so he walked up to a tanned girl in a red T-shirt and Levi's cutoffs.

"Are tryouts here?" he asked her.

She just stared at him.

"I said—"

She just stared some more, so he walked away. Then he saw a kid wearing a jersey and pads.

"Where do I sign up for tryouts?"

"Search me, dude." The kid walked away.

Rudy wandered over to the locker-room entrance. Soon a redheaded girl came up to him.

"You the guy with the bag of footballs?" She frowned, pulling his duffel bag from his shoulder. Some underwear fell out. "Very nice."

"I'm not a gofer or flunky," he said. "I'm a quarterback who's here for tryouts."

A sunburned player with NFL-sized shoulders came up to them and asked Rudy, "You sure you want to be here?"

"This is the only place I want to be."

Another Pioneer soon joined them. His helmet dangled from his fingers and the others smiled at him as if he had just won the Heisman Trophy. His jersey bore the number 12. Rudy knew what that meant: Quarterback.

"I'm here," Rudy told him, "to try out for the team."

"We're doing that right now." Then, "We went eleven-and-zero last year."

"Nice for you."

"We had about four seniors who graduated, and we had no trouble replacing them with juniors."

"More power to ya."

"If you were our coach, would *you* want you?"

"I would say, 'OK, let's see what you got.' And if this new guy could get the job done, I would say, 'Yeah, you're in.'"

"Well, they already have a guy who can get the job done." The kid tugged on his jersey.

The cheerleader said, "Mario here is almost as good as he thinks he is."

"I'm not dissing you," Rudy told him. "I'm just saying I think I should get a tryout."

The guy with massive shoulders glowered at Rudy. "Our perfect season last year? It was because of Mario. His dad—"

"Shut it, Grant," Mario said.

"I'm just saying that we have a great chance at going undefeated this year, too, as long as we have the right quarterback playing for us. Why do we need some new guy to be our quarterback? As the saying goes, 'If it ain't broke, don't fix it.'"

"Hey! What's all this jawin' about?" Coach Hartman bulled his way into the bull session. "Only one that should be talkin' out here is me."

"Got a guy here who wants my job, Coach," said Mario. "I was just explaining to him how it is."

"Oh? And how is it?"

"I'm the quarterback, that's how it is," Mario told him.

Coach Hartman was a medium-sized man with a remarkably muscular physique. He had a pleasant face and a Fu Manchu mustache.

"What's your name?" he asked the new guy.

"Rudy Maxa. I just moved here from out of state. I'll be a junior."

"What kind of football experience do you have?"

"I was junior varsity quarterback in Indy. We set a state record for total yards."

Mario snickered. "Indiana. Junior varsity."

"I know you have a winning team here, Coach," Rudy said, "and I respect that. I just want to get out there and show you what I can do. Maybe there's some way I could contribute to your team."

Hartman nodded. "I'm always looking for

someone to step up in case one of my boys gets hurt. I'll give you a tryout with the junior varsity. If you're as good as you seem to think, you'll play junior this year. Then next year, after my seniors have graduated, maybe you'll be my quarterback next year, too."

Rudy' asked, "Why not let me compete against the seniors this year?"

"Oh, all right. Suit up and show us what you can do."

"Coach! No!—" Mario's mouth dropped open.

Coach Hartman glowered. He shook his head. "Why don't these kids respect me anymore? Mario, get out there and start running. Lauren, show Rudy where he can get changed."

"Happy to." She took him by the hand and snarled at Mario. As she walked Rudy to the locker room, he said, "Are you and Mario a couple or something?"

"'Or something.' We're on and off."

"At the moment, what's your status?"

"Right now we're off."

"Why?"

"Because," she told him, "at the moment he seems to think that there's nothing more important in this world than football. Including me."

When they reached a door, she used her free hand to bang on it several times. "Whoever is in there, if you've got anything sticking out that I shouldn't see, better put it away because here I come!" To Rudy she muttered, "Like they have anything I've never seen."

She threw open the door and pulled him into the empty locker room. He set his duffel bag on the floor and said, "Thanks for your help."

"Nothin' to it." She plopped down on the bench.

"Uh, I'm gonna get naked now," he said.

"Nice for you."

"You just gonna stand there and check me out?"

She giggled. "I'm going." Then, "What's a good ol' boy like you from the Midwest doing way out here?"

"My mom got a job at the *Transcript*. I think what she really wants to do is take pictures of redwood trees, and California is full of them."

"What's your dad do?"

"He's back in Indy. That was part of my mom's decision to move here—she wanted to get away from him."

"Too bad." She stood up and left; his eyes followed the bounce of her lovely butt. *You're here to work, not play,* he told himself.

Outside, he saw Lauren and Mario standing together, pointing and glowering at each other.

"I could be making out with that dude and it wouldn't be any of your business, Mario. Who cheats on whom? Huh? Answer me that!"

Mario looked past her and said, "Hey, stud! They're ready to see what you can do."

Coach Hartman said, "Gonna start by having you throw a few basic patterns. OK?"

"Gotcha," said Rudy replied.

The new guy threw a pass at tight end Derry Lucas, who made no effort to catch a pass that landed about a foot from him. Then Arnie Calvin had to slow down to make sure Rudy's pass appeared uncatchable. Joey Rossi, the halfback, actually had to dance around Rudy to make sure he didn't receive the handoff.

"Hard luck," Mario said.

"I wouldn't give my squad an A for effort on that

one," Coach Hartman said.

"Maybe I just don't have my best stuff today," Rudy said.

"Oh, it's not *your* fault."

"I've been doing some, uh, independent training," Rudy told him. "By myself and with a pal." He thought with a grin back to his afternoon with Chuck at Burned Out Park. But his grin became a frown as he remembered how the old dude beat cheeks out of there after breaking that car's window. What a cowardly thing to do! Rudy had left a note on the windshield and was still waiting to hear from its owner. When that call came, Rudy could see himself saying to his mom, "I need to have someone's window replaced. Would you lend me a few hundred bucks...?"

Coach Hartman got his squad together and said, "Boys, we have here a new student named Maxa who wants to try out. So far you've dropped every pass he's thrown you, and I figure that's *your* problem, not his. So, for the rest of this tryout, if he throws you a catchable pass, you better catch it if you want to play for me this year. If he gives you a handoff, you better tuck it in just the way you would if Mario Mojo here gave it to you."

This time, Rudy again threw strikes and the players caught them, and his handoffs were impeccable. Mario stood nearby the coach and made a face as Rudy showed them what he could do.

The new QB knew he had some trouble when he noticed the whispering that seemed to be happening among the defensive players as they waited for the chance to rush him. He took the snap and stepped back into the pocket; his offensive line, there to protect him, collapsed like the flimsiest of toys, Rudy jumped backwards, seeing his opponents advance upon him with faces contorted in rage. His heart pounding in terror, he hurled the ball over their heads and it landed a dozen feet from his closest receiver.

The players rushing him, seeing his empty hands, ran past him and then walked around as a whistle blew. Rudy just stood there, alone and humbled. Humiliated, even.

Hartman shook his head. "You have a good arm, Maxa. We'll have to work on the rest. Lauren, would you fetch him a playbook?"

"Yessir."

"Maxa," he said, "you're going to spend some mighty long hours on the bench. This squad and I have been together for quite a little while now. We do most things well and a few things great. We function as a team, and you're the outsider for now. I'm not going to alienate my boys by giving you a bunch of playing time, regardless of how good you turn out to be."

"I understand that, sir."

Lauren came back with a manila envelope. "You need to sign for this, to prove that you got it."

"What if I refuse to sign?"

"I'll have to give you a spanking."

"Promise?"

Just then, Mario called out, "Lauren, the cheerleaders are all in the end zone. They need you."

"Tell them to chill. I'm going to walk Rudy to the parking lot."

She stayed out of the locker room this time. He half-wished she had insisted on going in and watching him change.

When they got to the parking lot, she pointed at his Passat. "That your ride?"

"'Fraid so."

"Nice. Still making payments on it?"

"Nope. My dad bought it for me so I would stay with him in Indiana. So I kept the car and moved out here anyway."

"So," she asked, "are you going to offer me a ride or what?"

"Get in."

She did as told. As they drove, he put down the car's top and admired how the wind blew through her long hair. He also observed how she kept watching Mario as he practiced. Mario was probably watching her, too.

"Should I feel offended that you're here with me now just to make him jealous?"

"You can feel any way you want about anything you want," she told him. "You did OK today out there."

"Yeah, just OK. I really threw the ball away at the end there."

"You lost your composure," she told him. "I'll bet you could go out there alone and hit targets all day, but when you've got a defender coming at you, you wig out."

"Sad but true. You think Hartman noticed that, too?"

"Uh, yeah. I kinda think he did."

CHAPTER 3

From his first day in football, Rudy had been told that he lacked the "edge"—the fearlessness that all quarterbacks needed to have. Even back in Indiana, the local media had mentioned that Maxa had all the qualities to become a first-rate quarterback except courage. Back in Indy, they had ragged on him plenty about that. What was the sense of suiting up for a game, they wanted to know, if he wasn't going to do his very, very best to get to the NFL and win Super Bowls? Don't even get out of bed if you aren't striving to go out there and dazzle the universe.

He went back to pass and threw a rocket that sailed through the California sky and struck the ground so hard that bits of beige grass went flying here and there. Rudy stood there and sighed. All by himself, he could throw the ball ten miles and hit targets, but that was worth zero if, in a real game with real opponents, he lost his nerve when the other side came after him.

Rudy stared at the motionless pigskin at the other end of the park, wishing it would roll over back to him. When it did not, he began traipsing over to it. Then he saw the big man climb the fence and join him in Burned Out Park.

I don't know what the deal is with this old guy. Maybe he's a pedophile and nobody his own age will have anything to do with him. Then he remembered something Mitch had said: *The best part of football is knocking the other guy on his butt.*

Yeah, the old guy could certainly do that.

"Hey," Rudy called out, "tackle me."

The big man nodded and charged at him. Rudy thought for a moment of a YouTube video he'd seen of a pit bull going after a heavily padded agitator. Mitch all but growled as he threw himself at Rudy and flattened the kid.

"I've gotta start wearing pads," Rudy said. "I hurt all over now."

"Get used to it." Mitch pulled him to his feet. "If you're gonna play football, you're gonna get banged up, and no pads will save you from that."

Mitch ran over to the bronze horse and sat in its saddle. "You're a wimp, kid. You'll have to toughen up some before you're ready to go pro."

"Call me Rudy. That's my name." Then, "Remember when you threw that pass and it broke that car's window? You ran off. I'm still waiting to hear from the owner. That's going to cost me some bucks."

Mitch shrugged. "Windows get busted. Arms and legs, too. Stuff happens."

"What happens next time you throw a pass and break someone's property? Will you expect me to pay for that, too?"

The old man glowered. "Don't get huffy. I'll pay you back."

"Well, when the owner calls me about getting his window replaced, how will I contact you? What's your phone number?"

"Don't you have it already?"

"Nope. You're Mitch from around the neighborhood. That's all I know about you."

"We'll exchange information later." He sat up on the horse and took a long look at Rudy. "You don't look so good. Your arm is turning every color of the rainbow. Better get some ice on it."

Mitch hopped off the horse and walked with Rudy a couple of blocks to a 7-11. The man entered the store and made a beeline for the freezer. He extracted a bag of ice and walked past the cashier as if he were at home.

Outside, Rudy said, "How come you didn't pay for that ice?"

"I will—when I get around to it." They sat at a nearby bench. "Here, you need to wrap the bag around your arm till you really feel the cold."

Rudy did so. He closed his eyes. "Ooh, feels good. Wish I had a bigger one for the rest of me. I don't know which part of me hurts the most."

Mitch stood up. "Gotta go. Later."

Rudy, startled, asked "How come? Where you going?"

"Got places to go and people to see." He started running.

After a few minutes, Rudy felt a little better. He went back inside the 7-11 and said, "That old guy left without paying for the ice."

The cashier chuckled. "That old Mitch! He's somethin', ain't he? He'd get around to payin', I'm sure."

CHAPTER 4

Most of the time, Rudy felt that his teammates kept forgetting he was there. To them there seemed to be two quarterbacks on their team, and the one who mattered was named Mario Cruncietti.

The only Pioneers player with any empathy for Rudy was Joey Rossi. "Mario thinks of you as a threat."

Rudy shook his head. "Not me. He's like King Midas around here. I'm just the new guy who's here in case Mario gets hurt, which I don't think is going to happen."

"Not just a football threat," said Joey. "A threat in other ways, too. Look over there."

Rudy looked. He saw Lauren practicing with the other cheerleaders. She was beautiful. He liked beautiful girls. He liked girls, period. Sometimes, they liked him back, and that was *rad*. He'd never had a steady girlfriend but hoped he would find one soon.

"Lauren told me she'd broken up with him."

"They've done that a hundred times."

As if overhearing them, Lauren hurried over to them and said to Rudy, "I saw you make some good moves out here. But remember to put all your weight on your left foot when you throw passes. You'll get more velocity that way."

Rudy grinned. "Thanks, Coach."

She grinned back. "Nothin' to it."

Practice ended at lunchtime. Rudy drove his VW while he devoured his Whopper and guzzled his Pepsi. Here in this arid California town, he always felt thirsty. His next stop, Burned Out Park, was where he hoped to find Mitch for more tacking and passing. Mitch, though, had his own schedule, and Rudy could never be sure if the old dude would be tardy or absent altogether; then there would be the occasional time when Rudy would arrive to find Mitch sitting on the horse, arms crossed, frowning at the youngster for not being there when the oldster was ready to play.

"Hey, Hoss! Where you been, havin' java with the mayor? I don't like to be kept waiting."

In the beginning, Rudy tried to get Mitch to agree to meet him at the park at a specific time, but that just didn't work out—Mitch would show up... whenever.

Rudy got annoyed sometimes, but he had to admit that not knowing when Mitch would arrive made their sessions together that much valuable to the boy. Rudy had no interest in practicing in the park by himself after being chased and challenged by Mitch.

The kid stood alone in the park, tossing his football into the air and feeling bored to death, when he heard a voice call out, "You!"

He turned around and saw a skinny old man standing at the northern entrance.

"Yeah?" Rudy called back. "Mitch?" He considered it weird that Mitch would come in through the north this time. Usually the old guy used the eastern entrance.

"Are you Rudy Maxa?"

"Yeah, that's me."

The skinny man turned around and walked away.

Rudy started after him. "Mitch! Where are you goin'?"

Then Mitch appeared, ten yards away. "Hoss, you just gonna stand there? Throw me the ball!"

Rudy nodded and fired a zinger right at Mitch's solar plexus, which might have knocked him unconscious if he hadn't gotten his hands up in time and made a perfect catch. "Nothin' wimpy about *that* one, Hoss."

Mitch threw it back in a high, soft arc—and charged at Rudy so that the teen would be knocked on his butt as soon as he caught the ball. Those hits were excruciating, but they were also much more real than the love taps that passed for tackles at Pioneers' practices. While his teammates seemed content to hit him and watch him fall, Mitch wrapped his arms around Rudy and drove him back and down.

Back in Indiana, Rudy had watched Peyton Manning throw passes and then throw *himself* to the ground to avoid being tackled. Rudy thought Manning was smart to do such a thing and not all cowardly. But for Mitch, the hit was the point of the game. He loved the *crunch!* of the tackle and the dozen or more ways this or that tackle could bring about a different result. Just as a professor's enthusiasm about his subject made his students more interested in his lectures, so too Mitch's passion for rough-and tumble football inspired Rudy.

"What's with all those cuts and bruises?" his mom asked. "In Indy, you didn't come home all banged up."

"That was different. Back then, I was playing against boys. Now my opponents are men."

Mitch was conscientious about tending to his beaten-up protégé. Often they exited the park to go to 7/11 for bandages, ice, rubbing alcohol and, it seemed, gallons of Gatorade.

Rudy admired how people on the street stopped by to say hello to Mitch, who was gentlemanly in return. But those visits were invariably brief and Rudy always felt afterwards that Mitch did not know precisely who those acquaintances were.

Mitch helped himself to whatever he thought he and Rudy might need or like—energy bars that, to Rudy, thought tasted like dog biscuits, ice-cold power drinks and ointments for sore muscles—and walked out the door without so much as looking in the cashier's direction.

"Don't worry about it," they said to Rudy. "He runs a tab. His wife comes by and pays it off. It's all good."

"Nice to know." He felt pleased to learn that Mitch had a wife. That made it less likely that the old guy was a park pervert who had weird designs on Rudy.

Occasionally, Mitch would end their Burned Out Park workouts by blurting, "I gotta split" or "Catch you later," and leave. Other times, he would just turn around and go home, saying nothing.

Occasionally, Rudy scratched his head at Mitch's abrupt departures from their afternoons. Perhaps it had started getting cold or Mitch was hungry and simply wanted to go home for dinner.

One day, Rudy said, "That's all for today. It's dinnertime, and my ma goes ballistic if I'm not home on time."

"Same here," he said.

"You mean your wife rags on you if you're not home on time?"

Mitch frowned. "Yeah, right, whatever."

Rudy went to the parking lot and stowed his gear in his VW's trunk. He thought, perhaps for the hundredth time, how lucky he was to have a car, especially a young man's vehicle. One thing he'd learned was that, especially in California, you were nobody if you lacked your own ride. Trouble was, having your own ride cost money, money, money.

"Rudy Maxa?"

Rudy turned around and saw the tall, emaciated man he'd spotted earlier. The guy wore a blue work shirt that said his name on an oval patch on the left breast. It said ELMER. He had sharp features and a mean face. Standing alongside him was a Claymore police officer.

"Yes, I'm Rudy Maxa."

"I knew it! He's the kid who busted my car's window!"

Rudy threw up his hands. "It was just an accident! I left a note! I'll pay for it!"

"He admits he did it!" The old guy reached into his pocket, pulled out Rudy's note and read it. "'Sorry I broke your window...my phone number is...'"

Rudy winced. "Oops."

The old guy snarled. "Yeah, 'oops' is right. You gave me the wrong number."

"I got our new one mixed up with our old one in Indiana."

"Is that so?" The guy smirked.

"Yeah, it *is*. I'm no liar."

The cop said, "OK, let's go to the station and check this out."

Kathleen Maxa went as fast as she could to the police station and sat down next to her son.

"I apologize for this," she said to the cop. "I'm sure we can fix this. Rudy has never been in trouble with the police—"

"He's not in trouble now. Just make sure you pay for that window and we'll consider the matter resolved."

"Sure, we can do that. You know, we've just moved here from the Midwest so I could take a job at the *Transcript*. We just want to mind our manners and get along."

The cop grinned. "That's the right idea." He reached over to shake her hand. "I'm Bruce Michaelson."

She smiled and shook it. "Kathleen Maxa. Rudy here just tried out for the Pioneers. He's a quarterback."

"I think we need a backup for Mario Cruncietti. Football is pretty dangerous."

Kathleen rolled her eyes. "Yeah, tell me about it. I've seen the footage of Joe Theismann and Darryl Stingley, and I just think, 'Oh! Could anything like that ever happen to my Rudy?'"

They left the station a few minutes later. Kathleen said, "Well, we'll pay for the window and put this behind us."

"The old guy? Elmer? He was such a mean old

fart. He wanted to have me thrown in jail! At least the cop was nice."

"Yes, he was. I hope you're minding the speed limit when you drive. There's no such thing as a cheap speeding ticket, just as there's no such thing as a cheap bill for a window replacement." Then, "How *did* you break that window anyway? Did the football go through the tire and out into the parking lot and break the window?"

Rudy shook his head. "Nothing like that. This other dude threw me a pass. I tried to catch it but missed and it sailed out of the park and hit the car."

"*'This other dude'?* What's his name?"

Rudy shrugged. "Search me, Mom. He's just some guy I met at the park. We throw the ball sometimes."

"Well, if 'this other dude' actually threw the ball that broke the window, shouldn't he kick in a few bucks to have it replaced?"

"Yeah, you're right. I'll call him and tell him to pay up."

Hearing the door open, a big black poodle barked and hurried over to welcome Mitch as he entered the house. "Wassup, Pierre?" he asked, stroking the dog.

A teenaged girl pecked him on the cheek and said, "Tell me about your day, Dad."

"I played football with Hoss till a cop came by and took him away. I'm thirsty." He went into the kitchen.

"Mario," the girl said, "did you hear what Dad just said?"

Mario looked up from the TV. "Nope, and I'm glad I missed it."

"I'm wondering if he's getting worse."

"Worse than what? On his good days, he can remember his own name. Don't get me started on his bad days."

"He's not as bad as that. You know what his problem is. The doctors have explained it all to us."

Mario let out a small, bitter laugh. "They know what it is, but they can't cure it. Doctors are useless."

"I hear ya." The girl then opened a can of dog food, emptied it into a plastic bowl and said to the poodle, "Trina, you must be hungry. Come have some dinner."

CHAPTER 5

"This school," Rudy said to Lauren, "is way too confusing. I still can't find my way from one classroom to the next."

"You'll figure it out soon enough. I guess you didn't have high schools like this one back in Indiana."

"Guess not. We also didn't have cheerleaders who flirted with us, then criticized the way we played."

She chuckled. "Well, football is a very competitive game—always ten players for every position. If I see a player who needs advice, I'll give him some."

"Mario needs no advice," Rudy muttered. "The guys on the Pioneers? They listen to Mario, not the coach."

"You weren't here last year. You don't know how it was. Last season was magic. Whole lotta magic."

"You mean because the team had a perfect record? There were high-school football teams all over America that were perfect last year."

She regarded him with gentle eyes. "Around here, we love our Pioneers, and occasionally they love us, too. Last year, it all came together for us—we went all the way. We broke a dozen records. It was *our* victory as much as it was the Pioneers'. So along comes this hotshot from Indiana who's, like, 'You won it all last year? Big deal. I want Mario's job.'"

Rudy stuck out his chin. "No way! I've never said such a thing!"

"Maybe not in so many words, but you started attending this school with, like, this *attitude*. Nobody appreciated it, especially Mario."

Rudy looked right and left. "Where *is* he, anyway? If you're here and I'm here and we're talking to each other, I have to think that he's close by, spying on us."

"Then let's give him something to see." She grabbed his arm, pulled him into the nearest classroom and kissed him.

"Ahem."

Rudy and Lauren kept their embrace going but opened their eyes and ended their kiss.

"Lauren," said the girl who'd just cleared her throat. "Mario would be *so* disappointed."

"Bag it, Kimberley. Don't tell him. Or *do* tell him. He doesn't own me. We broke up, you know."

"You two have broken up dozens of times. But you always get back together. Is Mario 'Mr. Right' while Rudy here is 'Mr. Right Now'?"

"Oh, Kimberley, please do tell me about boyfriends and dating and relationships," said Lauren. To Rudy she said, "You see, Kimberley has never been on a date."

"Too bad for Kimberley," Rudy replied.

"Too bad for *you*, Rudy," Kimberley retorted, "if you get mixed up with Lauren. If you don't believe me, just ask Mario about her." She shook her head and walked away.

"Friend of yours?" asked Rudy.

"Kimberley Cruncietti," said Lauren.

"Mario's sister?"

"Yep." Then, "You see, Mario has hot pants for everything in a bra, so whenever I've caught him with someone else, I would break up with him and Kimberley would blame me."

"So you guys have called it quits forever?"

She nodded. "This time I know it's for real." She added, "Many things have changed for me and Mario over the past year or so. Mostly him, though. He used to be fairly modest and humble for a Big Man on Campus. He also used to have everyone over to his house to watch TV, have rap sessions or just chill. But now he spends most of his time alone. I really don't what the deal is, but he's become this loner." She sighed. "Oh, well. Life goes on." Then, "Rudy, don't be a fool. Getting me to talk like this isn't going to get me into the backseat of your car."

"Huh?"

"Meet me after class and we'll pursue that matter in more depth."

Elmer the Exterminator, on Cedar Street, had a sign out front with a huge, very real-looking spider suspended on wires designed to look like a web. It freaked Rudy out as he parked his car and strode towards the front entrance.

"No! Not you!" Elmer said, scowling from behind the counter.

"Relax, sir. I come in peace." Rudy handed over his mother's check. "This should cover the window replacement."

"I hope this don't bounce like that football you used to bust my window."

"I'm sure it won't."

"Better not," Elmer mumbled, stuffing the check into his pocket.

"I'll be minding my manners from now on, and I hope you'll forgive me for this incident."

Elmer harrumphed. "You kids have no shame. You break people's property and say, 'Mommy, I need money to get this fixed.' Or you just run away and pretend it never happened."

"Well, I'm a kid who pays his bills. The few and the proud."

"Don't be a doofus."

"Hey! Give me a freakin' break!" Rudy felt his face redden. "I could have just busted your window and run off—and gotten away with it, too—but I didn't. I did the right thing. So how come you're ragging on me?"

"Because you have no respect for your elders!" Elmer pointed past Rudy. "Get out of my store and don't come back! And make sure your hoodlum friends stay away, too!"

Rudy threw up his hands. "What friends? What hoodlums? I'm new in town. Nobody knows me." He wheeled around and strode out of the store. He looked up and around. A beautiful day, a few clouds, a brisk breeze. He wished he was in the mood to enjoy it.

"Hey, Hoss. Psst."

Rudy looked in the direction of the voice. "Mitch?"

"Yeah. Why were you in that old fart's shop just now? He's such a doofus."

"Don't you remember? You threw the football, I couldn't catch it, it broke a car's window—*his* window. I gave him a check to cover the damage." Then, "I'm still waiting for your half."

"You'll get it."

"When?"

"You'll get it when you get it." Mitch wore a red T-shirt, gray sweatpants and sneakers. He had already sweated through his T-shirt. Rudy noticed, hardly for the first time, how muscular the old guy was. No gut, either. Rudy wanted to look that good at that age.

"I hope I get it soon."

"Got your football?" Mitch asked.

Rudy nodded. "In my car. Never leave home without it."

"I'll meet you in the park in fifteen minutes."

"Why not just ride there with me?"

"Because," Mitch said, "I like to jog."

Rudy shrugged. "Whatever turns you on."

Mitch pointed at the exterminator's shop. "I don't like him. I never have. Wanna do something about it?"

"No. If you do something, he'll blame me."

"I'm thinking of making his shop the local hangout for every insect in the Inland Valley."

"Don't tell me about it."

"I would go to Safeway and get lots of sugary stuff. Bugs love sweets."

"Didn't know that."

"Well, now you do."

So they ended up at Safeway. Mitch said, "All we really need is a bag of white sugar. Get a five-pound bag."

"OK."

Rudy got the sugar and as they walked out, the cashier looked at the bag of sugar and wrote something down. Rudy figured Mitch had a tab here, too.

"We can wait at the park till the old fart locks up for the night," Mitch said as they got into the VW.

Once they reached Burned Out Park, Rudy said, "I don't really feel like throwing the football right now, considering."

"Considering what?" asked Mitch.

"Considering what we're going to do with that sugar." Then, "Mitch, why is someone your age participating in someone else's retaliatory stunt?"

"It's not your stunt. It's mine. I thought of it."

"Why are we doing this?"

Mitch shrugged. "Why not?"

"We could get in trouble."

Mitch nodded. "Plenty of trouble. Vandalism is a felony."

Rudy convinced himself that what they were contemplating doing was highly regrettable. He needed to say, "No, Mitch, we're not going to destroy Elmer's store and go to prison." But he kept his mouth shut, mostly because he was still sore at Elmer over the way the exterminator had treated him and Mitch had a well-organized plan for getting even. Rudy thought back to Terre Haute, when one of the neighborhood bullies had gotten a secondhand car as a Christmas gift. Rudy and a few friends had sneaked out at about four in the morning and poured water into the bully's gas tank. A day or so later, the enraged bully started taking the bus to school again. Revenge,

Rudy concluded, could be as sweet as apple pie.

The two mischief-makers watched as Elmer locked up his store, climbed into his Buick and zoomed away. Rudy and Mitch sneaked up to the shop's front door. "Watch me," said Mitch as he began pouring fine lines of granular sugar around the entrance. He used his driver's license to narrow those lines.

"You look like a coke dealer," Rudy said.

"Hey, this stuff is cocaine for bugs. You ever do coke, Hoss?"

"Nope."

"Good. It's bad for your health."

"That's what they tell me." Then, "There are people around here. What if they catch us and call the cops?"

"They won't. Everyone here hates Elmer."

"Oh."

Mitch poured a large amount of sugar through the mail slot. "He opens tomorrow at ten. We'll come back just before then to check out his little infestation problem." The man cackled. "That bug man will think twice before he ever gets rude with anyone again!"

Rudy stepped back, surveyed Mitch's little prank and told himself he should think twice before he hung out with this old dude any more.

CHAPTER 6

His alarm went off, Rudy woke up, and the first words that popped into his head were: *What have I done? My God, what have I done?*

He wished he could get up, race over and clean up Elmer's place, then pretend the incident had never happened. But no, he didn't have that option. Rudy chided himself for participating in Mitch's foolishness—*What we did was as bad as arson or armed robbery! I can't believe it happened!*

Rudy went into the kitchen. His mother was already up.

"Go back to bed," she said. "It's Saturday."

"Why are *you* up so early?"

"Sometimes I get my best work done in the morning." She added, "Have you called your father lately?"

He poured himself a bowl of granola and drowned it in milk. "Not lately. Why?"

"Because," she told him, "he is your father, he bought you that car and I signed papers promising that you would call him. He called last night. You owe him."

"I'll do it," he said as he shoveled a mouthful of

milk and cereal into his mouth. "Or at least I'll email him."

"It's just as easy to call as email."

"You can call him after you're done eating."

"After I'm done eating, I have things to do."

His mother frowned. "Such as?"

I have to meet my weird old friend at the crime scene we created. "Just…things."

"Make time for your father. He's the only one you have. He cares about you. Pretend that you care back."

She loaded up her gear and left the house. He watched as she got into her SUV and drove off. As a *Transcript* editor, or whatever she was, she doubled as a photographer. Rudy admired his mother; or maybe just her enthusiasm for her job. She had worked as a journalist before getting married, and after Rudy was born, she became a stay-at-home mom. But after her divorce, Kathleen resumed her career with a determination Rudy had never observed in his mother. He'd been indifferent to everything—except maybe football and cute chicks. He had definitely been indifferent to his father, a man too busy making money to do much else. Rudy wanted to procrastinate on calling him because he believed neither of them had much to say that the other one wanted to hear.

After finishing breakfast, Rudy pulled on yesterday's clothes and got into his VW. He parked a block away from the crime scene, half-expecting to see three dozen cops and yellow tape everywhere.

The block was deserted. Rudy stuffed his hands into his pockets and sauntered up to the shop's front window and peeked inside. There he spotted a dark crawling mass that looked like a clip from some invasion-of-the-bugs movie. He looked away in disgust, yet smiled despite himself. Mission accomplished. How much would the old fart freak out when he saw this mess…and could he ever pin it on Rudy and Mitch?

The boy returned to his car and drove over to Burned Out Park. He looked around but could not find Mitch, so he lowered his car's roof, turned on the radio and blasted the air conditioner. Despite the early hour, Rudy felt hot. He loved the sensation of icy air blowing on his face, especially when he had music to enjoy. He guessed he would always fail to become a true Californian—too much of an aversion to sunshine and heat.

He opened an eye and checked the time on the VW's clock. Close to nine. Where was Mitch? The old dude could be late or absent when it came to football sessions at the park, but this was a different matter altogether. Getting even with Elmer seemed to give Mitch the deepest gratification, so why wasn't he here, grinning and chuckling like a six-year-old?

Rudy closed his eyes and thought, *Mitch and me, a couple of six-year-olds.* Such a notion gave him very little comfort.

CHAPTER 7

"Right there is perfect, Dad." Kimberley opened the Lexus minivan's door and smiled. "One good thing about living in a small town is that there's always somewhere to park."

"Don't be too long," Mitch told his daughter.

"Just gonna get my cell phone. Don't go wandering around, OK?"

He glowered at his daughter. "I'm not retarded."

"I didn't say you were."

"Maybe not in so many words, but you're treating me like a little kid, and I resent it."

"Sorry. No offense." She went into the store and hurried to the counter, watching her father in the car as she did so. She hated treating that way—as a little kid, or a retard, or whatever—but felt she needed to keep him under her thumb.

Her old cell phone had crapped out, so now she was getting a new one. She couldn't remember life without a cell phone and couldn't imagine how older folks had gotten through their days and nights without those priceless gadgets.

She took out her debit card, entered her PIN and thanked the clerk.

"Tell your dad I said hello," he said.

"OK." She wondered why nobody ever passed along good wishes to her mom.

The girl left the store, headed for the parking lot, and stopped. Her heart jumped into her mouth. The car was still there, but her father was not. He had even left the door open.

Rudy could see Elmer's craggy, humorless face through the windshield of the old guy's Buick as the big car cruised down the street, pulled into the lane past the huge spider and settled into a parking space.

The boy rolled his eyes. Mitch was going to be a no-show for Elmer's freakout!

But he looked again and smiled. There was Mitch, moseying along the street, whistling to himself as if everything were copacetic.

Rudy scrambled out of his VW and rushed to the older guy's side. "Mitch," he said in a loud whisper as he grabbed the man's arm and pulled him along. But Mitch pushed him away so hard that Rudy very nearly fell on his butt.

The kid tried again. "Mitch, it's showtime! He's gonna open the store!"

Mitch smiled and said, "For real? Let's go check it out!" The two sneaked over and hid behind a truck parked on the street in front of Elmer's store.

The boss had exited his Buick and now stood at his front door, going through his bundle of keys.

"There you are!" Kimberley shouted, running up from down the street. She eyeballed Rudy. "What are you doing here with my dad?"

Elmer unlocked his shop and went inside. Rudy

and Mitch made a queasy face at each other, imagining the little horror show crawling around on the floor in there.

"Ohhh! Nooo!" Elmer cried out as he got his surprise. He staggered backwards, out of the store, swatting at the area in front of his face.

Rudy and Mitch collapsed into each other's arms, laughing and crying in the quietest merriment.

Kimberley, her face livid, pointed at Rudy and said, "You're getting my father in trouble—"

"It's *his* fault!" Rudy retorted between gasps. "Your old man is corrupting me."

"Hahahaha," said Mitch, slapping Rudy on the butt.

"Enough of *this* crap." Kimberley reached over and grabbed one of her father's muscular arms. He did not resist. "Come on, Dad." To Rudy she said, "You don't understand him...how he is. My family is dealing with it. Just stay away. OK?"

Rudy wiped the tears from his cheeks, waiting for Mitch to give her what-for about coming along and spoiling his fun. But no; the big man just nodded and did as told. Elmer just stood there and tried to slap the vermin from his person.

Rudy took off, got back into his VW and drove to the park. He felt angry at Kimberley for telling him off, mainly because he agreed with her—he and Mitch had done a truly stupid thing. Looking back, Rudy had to admit that while Mitch had thought of vandalizing the store, Rudy could have said no, and meant it, and that would have been the end of it.

My name's Rudy. What's yours?
Mitch.
Mitch who?

Mitch Cruncietti, that's who. As in Mario Cruncietti's father.

Lucky guy, Mario. That explained way too much about Mario's athletic ability. What sort of sporting ability had Rudy inherited from *his* father? Zero.

Rudy turned on the radio, blasted the air conditioner and stared out at vacant Burned Out Park. Often he did his best thinking here. His father was a bossy, bullying money-is-everything kind of guy, so it was nice to be a couple of thousand miles away from him. Mitch in some ways was the kind of father Rudy wanted. Mitch's son Mario was a doofus, so that didn't say much for Mitch, and Mario's sister Kimberley was a ditz, which was to be expected considering her brother was Mario. If Missus Cruncietti was anything like her two progeny, no wonder Mitch spent so many hours at Burned Out Park playing football with Rudy.

The boy frowned, thinking of the hard push Mitch had given him just minutes earlier. The man played hard and hit hard in the park, but that push on the street? That was something more—a get-back-or-I'll-pound-you push. A moment or two later he became his former self, but that push, and the meanness behind it, made Rudy wonder about, and fear, his new friend. His only friend.

Rudy closed his eyes again thought: Mitch Cruncietti...where had Rudy heard that name? Maybe his new pal had played in the pros.

Hadn't Mitch's daughter said something like, "You don't know about my dad"?

Rudy decided he needed to check things out.

CHAPTER 8

Rudy did a Google search of *Mitch Cruncietti* and guffawed at the tens of thousands of results that popped up. He read the *Bay Area Times* article from February 25, 1993.

RAIDERS' "CAPT. CRUNCH" CALLS IT A CAREER

Mitch Cruncietti, 36, known in the NFL as "Captain Crunch," has announced his retirement from the Raiders after 17 seasons, all of them spent in Oakland. The 6'4", 255-pound linebacker finishes his career with 2,002 career tackles, including 780 solo stops, 23.7 sacks and a dozen interceptions.

Selected by the Raiders in the 1979 draft, Captain Crunch soon earned a reputation as a relentless competitor who craved opportunities to play as aggressively as possible against opponents. The player also became known as a practical joker who was loved and hated equally by teammates and players on other football clubs…

Whew! Rudy thought as he sat back and pulled at a lock of hair. Outrageous and unreal. He'd spent all those hours in Burned Out Park roughhousing with Captain Crunch, formerly of the Oakland Raiders. Certainly not a Hall of Famer, and not a terror like John Matuszak or Lyle Alzado, but a stable, solid defensive lineman just the same.

Figures. That's why he's so strong and aggressive and knows just the right way to tackle a guy. Plus, the Raiders and 49ers aren't that far away—I should have guessed right away that he had played for one of those teams.

The kid bet that Captain Crunch had made some better-than-decent money back then, too. Maybe not Peyton Manning-style megabucks, but a pretty sweet salary just the same, and a fat little pension, too.

So how come he's being so difficult about paying his share of the window he broke?

Rudy checked out the other items, most of which were about Mitch's performances in various games or fundraisers in which he had participated. To Rudy, reading about this guy was way too fascinating. Mitch owned two Super Bowl rings and in both games had been instrumental in keeping the other teams out of the end zone.

For several minutes the Claymore kid sat and stared at an online image of Mitch, airborne, taking out Troy Aikman as the quarterback prepared to throw the football. Captain Crunch had lost his helmet and Rudy chuckled at the sight of his friend's wild eyes and windblown hair.

Sometimes you can actually hear their bones crunch. Rudy wondered if Mitch could hear Aikman's bones break. The boy felt a renewed eagerness to get out to Burned

Out Park and mix it up some more with Captain Crunch.

"You're the boss right now, Maxa!" shouted Coach Hartman. "Act like it! Hear me?"

"Yessir!" Rudy shouted back. Hartman was always going on about how the quarterback ran the show—even if that guy was not named Mario Cruncietti—but Rudy that the Pioneers really had only one quarterback, and his name was *not* Rudy Maxa.

The snap was low and late, but Rudy pulled it in anyway. *One of the things about being a pariah,* he told himself, *is that if your teammates try to sabotage you, you're ready for it and can deal with it.*

Rudy's offensive line collapsed immediately and the pass rushers took off after the quarterback. These boys' reluctance to protect Rudy was equaled only by their eagerness to knock him flat on his back.

"Maxa!" hollered Hartman. "Stay in the pocket!"

And let these meatballs kill me? No, thanks. Rudy slipped two tackles and scrambled away like Fran Tarkenton. But he knew Hartman was right: the quarterback was going to get hit—that was simply a part of the game. The thing was, could he throw the pass before he bit the dust?

Surrounded by growling opponents, Rudy planted his feet, cocked his arm and threw a pass, then felt himself embraced and driven to the ground.

He lay on the for a moment, thinking, *My granny could hit harder than that, and she's dead!* The tacklers got off him and walked away without bothering to help him up. He also noticed that his intended receiver had made the catch and was sprinting into the end zone.

1

Hartman blew the whistle and all the players jogged over towards the 50-yard line. Rudy heard some applause and whistles from the stands.

"From here on out," Hartman called out to him, "try to stay in the pocket and look like a quarterback instead of running away like a pansy."

"Gotcha, Coach."

Presently he returned to the bench. At the Gatorade bucket, he said to Mario, "I didn't know Mitch was your dad."

"Yeah, I hear you two hang out at Burned Out Park every day."

Rudy nodded. "He's a great guy."

"You don't know him," Mario said. "Stay away from him."

Rudy frowned. "Because…?"

Mario frowned back. "Because I said so."

Rudy laughed. "Oh, yeah, well that settles it: I'm going to stop tossing the ball with your dad in the park *because you said so*." Then, "I'll tell you something, Mario: Since I've been here in town, your dad has been the only person who has bothered with me. Everyone else has treated me like a second-class citizen—including you. I have no idea how a fun guy like Mitch ended up with a couple of kids like you and Kimberley." He walked away, shaking his head.

In the locker room, Rudy felt sure that Mario and his pals would give him a hot foot in retaliation for what the new kid had said to the star. But they left him alone, and a few of the guys even praised him on his progress. *Maybe*, he told himself, *they weren't so bad after all.*

After he was done showering and toweling off, he heard girls' voices, so he checked it out by grabbing a chair, stepping on top and looking down over the transom window.

He saw Lauren. Whenever he got lonely and frustrated about moving from Indy to Claymore, he reminded himself that Lauren existed, and that she was here and not in Terre Haute, and he'd never met anyone quite like her back in the Hoosier State.

Rudy opened his mouth to say hidy when someone approached her. Mario.

"Thought you'd have gone home by now," Mario said to Lauren.

She shrugged. "Still here. You looked good out there today. You really moved around in the pocket."

Unseen, Rudy snarled at her. He'd thought he was the only one who got such feedback from her.

"Stop it," Mario said. "If I want to hear about how I did, I'll ask Hartman."

Lauren smiled. "It's football season. You need all the help you can get."

"Come on," he said. "I'll drive you home."

"Negative. I've got some stuff to do here."

Rudy grinned. How often did Mario Cruncietti get shot down, especially by his former squeeze?

"Are you waiting for something? Or *someone*?"

Lauren stuck out her chin. "Meaning…?"

"Your new friend," he replied through gritted teeth.

"Do you mean Rudy Maxa?"

"Duh."

"Well, what's it to you if I'm dating him?"

"Are you trying to get back at me for something?"

"Nope," she said. "Just spending time with people I like." Then, "The fact that you resent it makes it that much more satisfying to me. Besides, I have a weakness for quarterbacks. Remember?"

"But *that* guy? He's a wimp."

"*Is* he? You should check him out sometime. Do you remember the beginning of last year? You were as green as a football field."

Mario stalked off. Rudy got off the chair and finished dressing. Then he went down the hallway where she still stood. She wrapped her arms around his so that they clung together.

"Drive me home," she said.

"What's your address?"

"Doesn't matter. We'll just get into your VW and go and go. Sooner or later we'll pass by my place and I'll get out."

They walked in the general direction of the parking lot. Rudy asked, "What's the deal with Mario and his dad?"

She made a face. "Wrong question, dude. Here you are, arm in arm with the cutest chick in the entire Inland Valley, and you're asking me about Mario and his dad? Bad idea. You're supposed to be doting on me and turning me on."

"Like I said, what's the deal with those people? I thought at first that only Mario hated me, but his sister Kimberley has the same attitude."

She sighed. "Everyone our age has conflicts with their parents. Right?"

He nodded. "I moved two thousand miles to get away from my father. I'm as ashamed of him as he is of me. But Mitch? What a fun guy! He played in the NFL and loves to share his football wisdom with me. If he was my dad, I'd brag about him to everyone who would listen. But Mitch seems to be, like, 'Stay away from him and don't talk to him!' I don't understand that."

"Mario is very proud of him," said Lauren. "His whole family is. Mario and his dad used to be real tight—I don't know what changed between them, and Mario isn't too eager to talk about it. Maybe it has something to do with last season's perfect season. Mario is under a huge amount of pressure to go perfect this season, and I guess that pressure freaks him out sometimes. But you should be grateful that Mario is too preoccupied with everything to bother with me, and that's why I'm here with you now."

They reached his VW and got in. Lauren said, "I know Mario isn't one of your pals right now, but you need to say, 'I'm just going to do my thing and not let anyone's hostility get to me.'"

"Whatever you say."

They drove away and she gave him directions. Soon they reached her home, and in her driveway was a Claymore police cruiser. Leaning against it was Officer Bruce Michaelson.

"I had a feeling I would find you here, Rudy," the cop said.

CHAPTER 9

Kathleen Maxa walked into the police station and said, "Long time, no see, Officer."

Michaelson smiled. "The *Transcript* has been fun to read since you came along. I always look for your stories when I go online." Then, I'm afraid your boy here has been naughty again."

Kathleen frowned. "Rudy, what have you done now?"

Rudy shrugged. "Ask him."

So Michaelson explained to her the incident at the exterminator's shop and Rudy's probable involvement in it. Finally, Rudy looked up at his mother.

"I helped, but it wasn't just me, Mom. There was this other guy—it was mostly his idea."

"Another guy?" she asked. "What was his name?"

"I can't tell you."

"You *can't* or you *won't*?" the cop asked. "You see, I believe you, but until you give me the other guy's name, I have to treat it like you acted alone. Was it that girl from school?"

"Lauren? No. No way."

"Rudy," said Kathleen, "you're protecting this

other person, and you could get in big trouble over this. Is the other fellow the one who broke the old man's car window?"

Rudy kept his yap shut.

"Don't be a doofus," the cop said. "Don't make me charge you the only offender in this thing."

"How much trouble would he be in," Kathleen asked, "if you charge him with what happened at the exterminator's shop?"

The cop paused. "In this case, not much. The victim handled the mess himself—he's a professional exterminator with a real bad infestation problem in his own shop! He becomes his own customer, right? If he can't take care of business in this matter, he'll look incompetent, and ole Elmer is a mighty proud fella." To Rudy he said, "You've already paid for that broken window, so don't sweat it. But Elmer is a crabby old fart who's mad at the world and always looking for a fight, so stay away from him."

"OK. I hear ya."

Officer Michaelson said to Kathleen Maxa, "Make sure he minds his manners. Very nice to see you again."

Rudy thought the cop wanted to add, *I really, really would like to see you on my own time. How about dinner sometime?*

"Listen," the mother told her son once they were home, "I want to know: Did that girl Lauren help you dump that sugar in the man's store?"

"Negative."

"Then who?"

"No comment. All I can tell you is that I don't know him that well but I know he isn't a Blood or Crip. He isn't a crackhead or meth dealer or gangbanger."

Mitch is just a retired lineman whose adolescent children treat him like a retard. The big man may have had some growing up yet to do despite being fiftysomething years old, but no adult deserved to be treated like a mental midget. Nobody.

CHAPTER 10

"You're playing safety today, Maxa."

"Why, Coach?"

"Because that's where we need you. In case you haven't noticed, we've already got the best quarterback in the whole Inland Valley, so that sort of makes you redundant. What we need is a safety, so you're the guy."

"Yessir." Rudy's heart sank, but he knew how things were: You tried out for the position you wanted but took whatever they offered you.

The team's countless fans packed themselves into the stands butt to butt, and Rudy wondered how any of them could breathe. These folks, loud and proud when praising their Pioneers, all but shouted *You the man!* at Mario, and Rudy thought, *No wonder that guy is so full of himself. Everyone's kissing his butt all the time.*

As the cheers and applause began to subside, a deep voice became more audible. Rudy looked around and spotted Mitch. Naturally, the old guy had shown up to watch his son the quarterback. Beside Mitch stood a tall, thin, passably pretty blonde; was she his missus? If so, did she pay his tabs around town, and would she pay Rudy her husband's share of the window-repair bill?

He remembered a recent session at Burned Out Park with Mitch, their first time together since Rudy learned about Mitch's years as a Raider.

"I didn't know you were 'Captain Crunch.' That *was* you, right?"

"Yeah, whatever." Mitch then climbed onto the horse statue and lost himself in his own pleasant thoughts. Rudy guessed that Mitch just didn't like talking about his NFL days. Maybe the guy had good reasons for feeling that way—a weirdo out there, wanting to get his name in the newspapers, may have threatened Mitch's life at some point. Rudy knew that people in public life had to cope with those kinds of dangers.

Playing safety wasn't much fun, because the Pioneers didn't really need a safety; whenever the other team—the Jokers—ran a rushing play, the Pioneers' defensive line stopped the runner practically at the line of scrimmage, and most of the time the Pioneers' cornerbacks swatted away the Jokers' passes. With nothing much to do, Rudy did his best simply to look busy out there. On a pass play, he ran over to assist the cornerback and very nearly made an interception. The ball slid into and out of his hands.

"Good effort, Maxa!" Coach Hartman hollered. "Next time, wipe the grease off your hands and maybe you'll hold onto the ball."

Mario shook his head. "I can't believe he dropped the ball. It was right there."

"Grab some wood," Hartman said. Mario skulked back to the bench.

Rudy felt badly about the botched interception but didn't believe it made much difference one way or the other. The Inland Valley High Jokers could not play the Pioneers' kind of football and by the second half had stopped trying.

The clock went down to zero, and the crowd cheered some more. Rudy guessed that most of the fans couldn't remember the last time their team had lost, and the next several games would be easy victories. The stands emptied out as the friends and family members hurried over to greet their heroes.

Kathleen Maxa said to Rudy, "I brought my camera and got some terrific images. They'll be online tomorrow."

Rudy figured those images would be of Mario, not him. He looked over and saw Mario with Mitch and the blonde lady, smiling and talking. Then Mitch left them and ambled over to Rudy.

"Hoss," he said, "you played some good football out there. I know you wanna be quarterback instead of safety, but you did your best out there anyway. That shows character."

"Thanks, Mitch." Then, "I think Mario wants you back. He's starting to snarl at us."

"Oh, yeah, see ya." He wandered off, smiling.

CHAPTER 11

Mitch decided that one thing Rudy needed was more practice catching punts, so they did just that—Mitch kicked them halfway to the sun, and Rudy caught them. Then Mitch tackled him.

After a couple of hours, Rudy's hair and T-shirt were drenched, but he kept at it. He took plenty of hard hits from Mitch, but once in a while got one in, too, and soon realized that he craved the hits and pain. Rudy even thought of his hit-and-be-hit sessions when he was supposed to have his mind on other things like what his instructors were writing on the board or how Lauren breasts might feel in his hands, if that ever happened (as he surely hoped it would). Mostly, he just looked forward to the next time he would meet up with a brick wall named Mitch.

For Rudy, nothing was nearly as difficult as catching a football that was in something other than a spiral. He pulled it in and trapped it against his body, then braced himself for Mount Cruncietti. The big man slammed a shoulder into Rudy's upper arm, and the boy yelped in excruciating pain, as if an elephant had decided to sit on him.

Even an NFL assassin like Mitch had to

acknowledge that something had gone horribly wrong.

"What's the matter, Hoss? Tell me where it hurts."

"My shoulder! My shoulder! It's busted! Agggghhhhhh!"

Mitch shook his head. "Not busted. Just dislocated. Hurts like a bugger, don't it?"

"Agggghhhhh!"

Mitch reached down and pulled Rudy to his feet as if the young man were a rag doll.

"I'm gonna barf!" Rudy said, swallowing hard.

"No. What you're gonna do is relax and let me pull your bad arm nice and slow till the bone pops back into place. It's gonna hurt even more than it does already."

"Then don't do it," Rudy said, whimpering. "Just get me to a doctor. Get me to a hospital."

"Hoss, the only way to fix this thing is like I said—pop it back into place. I'll do it or a doctor will."

Rudy closed his eyes, wincing. "Got a car? Go get it and take me to Inland Valley Hospital. Hear me?"

Mitch nodded. "I'll be back in fifteen minutes."

Rudy staggered off to the biggest nearby tree with the best shade. He sat down with much care and leaned against the huge tree, doing his best to keep from retching.

Come on, Captain Crunch! Move your butt!

If anything, the pain grew worse as he sat and waited. He lost consciousness a couple of times, then woke up, wondering why Mitch hadn't come back. He looked up and around, noticing the sun's lower position. He checked his watch—he'd been sitting in pain for over an hour.

You're too late, Mitch. Looks like I'm going to have to

rely on Number One.

Rudy got up. He knew he was too weak to drive, and there was nobody here in hot, dry Burned Out Park to help him. So with his injured arm he got a gentle but firm grip on one of the lower branches of the big tree and closed his eyes as he pulled at the branch. He could hear himself scream, louder and louder, until he could sense nothing but his own agonized voice. Then everything went black. When Rudy opened his eyes again, discovering his shirt covered with vomit and the pain largely gone from his shoulder, he observed that Mitch had still failed to return.

I've had it with you, dude. Our friendship, or whatever it was, is officially over.

Rudy headed over to his car and switched on its engine, blasted its air conditioner and turned on satellite radio. He cruised out of the park, muttering about what a doofus Mitch was and what a fool Rudy had been to think they were friends.

Maybe I was better off back in Indy.

As he got closer to home he saw a tan-colored Lexus minivan coming his way. Rudy spotted Mitch behind the Lexus' steering wheel and waved hello. Mitch looked straight ahead and zoomed right past his Burned Out Park buddy.

Hey! What's up with that? Didn't you see me? Or maybe you did. We need to talk about this, big guy.

Rudy slowed down, made a U-turn and chased after Mitch. When tooling around town, Rudy had few chances to dog out his VW, but his car was built to *perform*. Within minutes he began tailgating the Lexus and waving for Mitch to pull over.

Amazingly, the driver did.

"Where were you today?" Rudy felt his face go red. His armpits felt flooded. "You were supposed to drive me to the hospital!"

Mitch cocked his head. "Huh?"

"You know what I'm talking about. You left me in the park with a dislocated shoulder. I barfed on myself." He pointed to the ugly stain on his shirt.

"Dislocated shoulder?" Mitch paused. "You need to pop it back into place—"

Rudy nodded several times. "Yeah, you told me that at the park. I did what you told me to do."

"Then your shoulder's fixed. What's your problem, Hoss?"

"Quit calling me that!" Rudy wiped some sweat from his face and scowled at his friend. "I've told you my name a dozen times, so don't pretend you don't know who I am. Also, I'm still waiting for you to pay me for that broken window. You owe me money!"

Mitch scowled. "I don't owe you nothin'! You're just tryin' to give me a hard time!"

Rudy threw up his arms and said, "I give up, Mitch. You win. Keep your money." He hustled back into his VW, cranked up the music and air conditioning and sped off, hating himself again for being foolish enough to try making friends with Captain Crunch.

Mario hadn't looked—really *looked*—at the poster of his father in some time. For years, the huge picture of Mitch Cruncietti, number 88, had been among Mario's most prized possessions, hanging on his bedroom wall. Mario had scrutinized the image hundreds of times—Captain Crunch in his Raiders uniform, kneeling, staring at the camera with his steely, fearless gray eyes. Mario had often thought that he and his father looked alike but could never convince himself that either male was handsome. Nor could he make himself believe that he had half of his father's courage.

My dad is, or at least was, Mitch "Captain Crunch" Cruncietti of the Raiders. Teammate of Jim Plunkett, Marcus Allen, John Matuszak, Lyle Alzado. Winner of two Super Bowl rings. What do I want from life? I want to become an NFL quarterback. That's it; I don't particularly want anything more. Problem is, while they say I'm the best football player in the whole Inland Valley, I know that doesn't mean very much. In the state of California alone, there are probably a thousand other guys my age with my level of skill.

Maybe I should have a Plan B.

"Mario!" called his mother.

"I'm real busy with something." He stared at the poster some more, wondering if he could endure all his father had had to put up with to get those two Super Bowl rings that now sat in their safety deposit box.

"If I have to come up there—"

Mario bounded down the stairs and saw his mother nearly shaking with rage. Behind her, Kimberley stood smiling, always in the mood to see their mom rag on Super Mario.

"How may I help you?"

"This way." She led him out to their driveway and pointed to the moderate dent in their Lexus' rear bumper. The vehicle sat there askew, as if having been parked by someone in alcoholic psychosis. "Want to talk about this?"

Mario laughed. "I never use the Lexus. That's

yours. I've got mine." He took a closer look at the bumper. "Could've been much worse. Maybe you went shopping and someone in the parking hit you and drove off without leaving a note." He shook his head. "Some people are just too rude."

"I haven't used the minivan all day," said the mother. "That dent didn't get there all by itself."

"I'm sure Mario didn't cause the damage," Kimberley put in. "Even *he's* a good enough driver not to hit anyone."

Missus Cruncietti threw up her hands. "Then who did it? Did someone steal the Lexus, bang it up, then bring it back? Uh, I don't think so."

Just then they heard the cheers from some sports event on the TV in the living room. Mitch had turned up the volume, as if wanting to drown them out.

Mario asked, "What about Dad?"

"What about him?" retorted his mother.

"Does he still drive?"

"He drove me to get my cell phone," said Kimberley.

"It's all right for him to drive if there's someone with him," said Missus Cruncietti.

"Claymore is small enough," said Kimberley, as if her town's modest size were a flaw requiring urgent correction. "He can walk wherever he wants to go, and the only place he wants to go to is Burned Out Park. Lord knows what he does there."

Their mother let out a big sigh and walked into the kitchen. She took the set of Lexus keys from the nail upon which they hung and put them in the back of a drawer they seldom used.

CHAPTER 12

Rudy terminated his relationship with Mitch, which was one of the easiest and most difficult things he had ever done. He disliked Burned Out Park's dry, wheat-colored grass and felt little regret about spending his afternoons elsewhere. Still, he missed Mitch and their camaraderie.

He shook his head in disgust. What kind of teenaged fool makes friends with a fiftysomething troublemaker who ignores debts, sabotages private property and says, "What are you talking about? I haven't done anything wrong!"? When Mitch banged up Rudy's shoulder and left him there with just a fake promise to return with help, the kid, if his arms had worked right, would have wrung the old fart's neck. So why had the youngster spent so much time with Mitch?

Maybe, Rudy thought, *our friendship happened because back in Terre Haute I had been a reasonably popular guy, but here in Claymore nobody had much use for me, so I chose to hang with the only guy who would hang with me, even though he was old enough to be my father.*

There was also the thrill of practicing with a retired Raider. Rudy had always concluded his practices with the Pioneers feeling that his teammates were boys trying to play a man's game. Mitch, however, gave him—and taught him to give back—NFL-quality hits. He wanted some more of that, but knew the only game in town offering such action was at Burned Out Park, and he'd already blown *that* stuff dead.

At practice with the Pioneers, Rudy thought those kids hit like pansies and he hit like Mitch.

"Good work, Maxa," Coach Hartman shouted. "The rest of you, watch Maxa. Remember, you're at football practice, not a square dance."

Later on, Lauren said to him, "You don't block like the other quarterbacks I've seen."

"That's because those others are just boys."

"You've improved, Maxa," the coach said.

"Doing my best, Coach," Rudy replied.

"Well, from now on you're my fullback. I want you to block for my boys."

Rudy discovered that he liked blocking. The boys he played against were as soft as marshmallows compared to Mitch, and Rudy helped create gaping holes that the Pioneers' running backs darted through. They gained so much yardage with their rushing game that Hartman decided to do one running play after another, which angered Mario. Rudy loved it; if he couldn't throw the passes and be the hero, the next best thing was to take away much of Super Mario's glory and fun.

Mario really felt out of sorts with this new strategy. After a half-dozen consecutive handoffs that brought them first downs, he took the snap, went back to pass and groped the pigskin as if he were just learning to throw the football. Hartman didn't seem to notice or care; to him, whatever worked, worked, and he was quite happy to have his quarterback hand off the ball as long as they got first downs and ended up with touchdowns and victories. Lauren, however, knew her ex, knew football, and knew that something was wrong even though everything seemed very, very right.

Rudy got spooked by the sight of Mitch in the stands. He kept looking and got more spooked each time. The old guy had really gotten to him and made him a better football player than he thought he could become.

Mario marched up to him on the sideline. "What's your problem, Maxa?"

"No problem here, dude."

"Then how come you keep eyeballing my dad? You got a crush on him or something?"

"No, man, he's not my type." Rudy felt embarrassed that even Mario knew how often he'd been shooting looks at Mitch.

"Here's your warning, Maxa. Get your selfie with him, if that's what you want, then stay away. Understand?"

"It's a free country, in case you haven't noticed. You can't tell me what to do."

"No?" Mario gave Rudy a hard shove, and the new guy went stumbling into his teammates. Hartman hurried up to them and pointed at Rudy.

"Maxa, take a powder!"

"Me?"

"Yes, you. Shoo."

Rudy shrugged, then traipsed to the locker room, calling Hartman names under his breath. He had blocked his tail off and created grand opportunities for his team's rushing game, and now he'd been banished to the showers. How unfair was that? he asked himself as kicked off his cleats.

Soon he heard the rustle of pompoms and looked up to see Lauren.

"Better get back out there," he muttered. "Game's not over yet."

"Two-minute warning and we're up by three touchdowns," she replied. "They don't need me." She smoothed out her skirt and smiled. Always the optimist, Rudy thought. He wondered if she would always be full of giggles, wiggles and jiggles. They were sitting in a guys'-only room, but nobody ever asked her to leave. Rudy let her stay. "You played great football today."

"Then how come he sent me in here?"

"Don't take it personally. Everyone notices great blocking. So do I. I notice nice tight butts, too."

"Do you like quarterbacks who lose their nerve in the pocket?"

She frowned. "Mario? Yeah, he's a little afraid of getting hit. But as long as he keeps winning, well, that's all that matters." Then, "Are you going to the party tonight?"

"I didn't know there was one."

"Well, now you know. It's at Grant's place. He lives in the biggest house in town and his folks are away for the weekend."

"Well, I wasn't invited."

"*I'm* inviting you. You can be my date," she said.

"Oh, Mario will love that."

"Too bad for him. Anyway, I've been to Grant's house lots of times, so I know all the best places there where we can sneak off and be alone."

He smiled and pulled her close. "What shall I wear?"

Grant Miller lived in the wealthier part of Claymore, in a big stone house that was much better than Rudy's home. He reminded himself that this *was* California, not terribly far from Silicon Valley and its megabucks.

Grant's house was all lit up and Rudy could hear the thump of dance music even as he drove up with his car's windows rolled up. As he got out of his car and walked towards the front door, he heard the sounds of love from within the abundant shrubbery.

"Who's there?" Rudy asked.

"Bounce," said the voice. Then, "Is that you, Maxa? It's too dark for me to see."

"Yeah, it's me. You're Joey, right? Wouldn't you two be more comfy in the house?"

"Doin' just fine out here."

The girl keeping company with Joey in the shrubbery said, "Hi, Rudy. You did some *awesome* blocking today."

"I would rather have thrown some awesome passes, but you can't have everything."

She said, "Rudy, does Mario know you're here? Just wondering."

"Why do you ask?"

"Well, it's just that he's going to get here any minute and see your car, and he's probably assuming that Grant didn't invite you but you showed up anyway...Mario has noticed that Lauren likes you, and although they've sort of broken up for the time being, he's still horny for her and may want to punch you out if he sees that you and Lauren are getting too friendly."

"He'd try to punch me out?" Rudy swallowed a small, bitter laugh. "Are you kidding? After all the blocking I did for him today? He should be full of gratitude."

"Mario's not into gratitude," Joey told him. "Either go home or go inside and stay out of everyone's way."

"So those are my options, huh? I think I'll go inside and say hello."

"Enter at your own risk."

As Rudy made his way to the double front doors, one of the doors flew open and out stepped his teammate Alvin Calverts, a golf club in his hands. Alvin, swaying and drooling, swung the club at Rudy, who stepped away from him and ducked into the house.

I hope you have a real bad hangover tomorrow morning, Calverts, Rudy said to himself as he entered the large foyer. He, of course, had been to plenty of football parties back in Indy, but those people were hicks; who knew nothing of decadence and debauchery. Here at Grant's house, the air reeked of beer and sweat and the loud music made Rudy's bones vibrate. The house was packed with dancing kids who looked as if they were auditioning for a porno video.

As soon as Grant, the host of the party, saw Rudy, he scowled and shouted, and even made obscene finger gestures with both hands, but the music was so loud and the crush of bodies so stifling that Rudy felt sure nobody else noticed Grant's little display of bad manners. Rudy smiled and waved, then darted past some dancers and tried to find Lauren before anyone else tried to confront him. All Lauren had to do was say "He's my date" and nobody would dare ask him to leave.

A crowded house made his search for Lauren more difficult. He took fifteen minutes to squeeze his way into the den, where a dozen or more kids cheered on a couple of girls as they felt each other up.

Rudy felt big strong hands on his shoulders. Then he felt himself being spun around. He saw Grant's big ugly face.

"Why are you here, Maxa? You weren't invited."

Rudy smiled. "But I *am* here and it's a great party."

Grant thrust out his chin. "Maxa—"

They heard screams as the two girls in the den started pulling each other's hair.

"No! No!" Grant pushed past everyone and tried to separate the two hair-pullers. Rudy pushed past everyone and made it down to the basement, where a few boys were whipping around a Frisbee that kept hitting partygoers in the head or shattering the crystal glasses sitting behind the bar. Rudy wondered what the man and lady of the house would think once they got home and saw this mess—unless by some miracle their son would get it all cleaned up in time, which Rudy seriously doubted would happen. Or perhaps Grant's folks, the most rabid of Pioneers fans, were so thrilled that their son and his team had a perfect record that they would consider a trashed house a minor nuisance. Pioneers football seemed to be the only thing that these Claymore people seemed to give a crap about.

Rudy ducked the Frisbee as it whizzed by and pushed past a couple making out. A pair of arms snaked around his waist, and he wondered if Grant had caught up with him. If so, the guy was getting just a bit too friendly for Rudy's liking.

But no. Grant didn't wear plastic bracelets.

"Glad you could make it," Lauren said as she rested her head on his shoulder. "If you'd stood me up, I would've felt hurt. I been hurt a lot, you know."

Rudy grinned. "Poor baby."

"You're such an Okie. Have you ever been to a California party?"

"Nope. Please tell me what to say and do."

She led him past some dancers to an isolated room and turned off the light. "I'll show you what California girls like to do at parties."

Rudy closed his eyes and felt her body pressed to his. Then he felt her lips on his and did whatever she was doing—he certainly didn't want her to think he was inexperienced at this sort of thing, although of course he was. She pulled him down onto a bed piled with blankets.

He had complained every other day to his mother about their move to Claymore, but at this moment he was feeling pretty good about things. Mostly he had found his life in Claymore to be unsuccessful, but these minutes with Lauren in the darkness rendered all of his grievances against the universe—real or imagined—irrelevant.

Rudy had so completely forgotten about everyone and everything that he nearly had a heart attack when the door swung open and the light went on. Rudy and Lauren separated and tried to smooth out their clothes.

"Mario!" Lauren blurted, hiding behind Rudy.

"Yeah, it's me. I've come to wish you a good evening." He threw a punch at Rudy, who easily blocked it and threw one of his own. Presently the two football players began circling each other as if in boxing match.

The Pioneers' middle linebacker, Neil something, came in and broke it up.

Lauren shouted, "Mario, I invited Rudy to this party, so don't get mad at him! Get mad at me!"

"I'm mad at both of you."

"Well, don't start beating up on Rudy—"

"You don't have to stick up for me," Rudy said. "I'm not afraid of this guy." To Mario he said, "If you want a piece of me, here I am. Have you ever been in a fight?"

"What's that supposed to mean?"

"Just like I said. I don't think you've ever been hit in your life."

Mario glowered at him. "You shouldn't have come here tonight, punk."

"Oh?" Lauren interjected. "Do *you* own this house, Mario? I don't think so. And you *certainly* don't own *me*, although you always walk around acting like you own everyone and everything in sight."

Mario swallowed hard. "That's not me. I've never treated you that way."

Lauren put her hands on her hips. "How do you think you've treated me? Tell me. I'd love to hear about it."

Just then Joey entered the room. "Hey, guys! What's with all this fighting? Last time I checked, parties were supposed to be fun!"

Mario pointed at Rudy. "He's not supposed to be here. He wasn't invited. I was just telling him to bounce."

"Seems to me," Joey said, "that he's on the team. He has a uniform and a playbook. It doesn't do much for our team spirit if you two start beating up on each other."

"Where was Maxa last year, when we had a perfect season and *Sports Illustrated* wrote about us? He was still in Okie-land. Coach brought him on board and said, 'Maxa's in.' But this Cracker is not one of us and never will be."

Rudy, who had never been called "Cracker" until now, tried not to be offended by the slur as he looked around and tried to figure out whose side everyone was on. But he couldn't tell; still, no one was grabbing his by the arm and hustling him out of Grant's house.

Joey said, "Think fast!" as he tossed a can of Pabst Blue Ribbon at Rudy, who caught it, opened it and took a long drink. *My mom would go ballistic if she saw me drinking.* He didn't especially like the taste of the stuff, but needed to show them he was one of the boys.

"Mario!" Joey tossed a beer to the quarterback, who snatched it out of the air and nodded unsmiling at his teammate.

Rudy put his can to his lips for another unwanted sip when the lights began flickering on and off. Within moments, someone turned down the deafening music so that normal conversation would be possible.

"Mario!"

The boy whirled around. "Kimberley? Bounce, kid. This is no place for you."

She stood on the landing, her breathing ragged as she pulled at her hair. She hurried down the stairs and up to her brother and began whispering to him.

"Dad needs me? What for? Where's he gone now?"

"Is Mitch in trouble?" Rudy said.

Mario darted at Rudy and tried to tackle him until Neil the middle linebacker stopped him.

"I warned you, Maxa!" Mario yelled as Neil held him back. "He's none of your freakin' business!"

Rudy broke out into a cold sweat. He knew that Mitch could be quite a handful to look after, and Mario and Kimberley were understandably fretting about him all the time. Kimberley stood there, practically shaking with anxiety, and Mario seemed preoccupied with many things aside from catching his on-and-off squeeze with Maxa at this party. It sounded to Rudy as if Kimberley had come by to tell her brother that their father had become a "missing person," but Rudy had seen the man at the football game a few hours earlier, so Mitch couldn't have strayed very far. Mitch had gone off to the park for several hours at a time to work out with Rudy, so why were his kids tripping out about his absence now?

Then Rudy felt as if a light bulb his head had suddenly flashed on. Mitch's kids had a right to worry about their father. Rudy had considered him weird and impulsive, aloof and indifferent; now he understood that the man was mentally ill.

"Gotta bounce, guys," Mario said, walking away with Kimberley.

"I'm going with you," said Rudy.

Mario turned around, gritting his teeth.

"I can help," Rudy told him.

Joey stepped in front of him. "Bad idea. It's their problem, not yours."

Lauren said, "Sorry, Rudy. I thought the party would go better than this."

He shrugged. "Doesn't matter."

But it *did* matter. The party had lost all of its

energy and momentum, and not even Lauren could make it fun again for Rudy—if, in fact, it had ever *been* fun.

So Mitch's kids didn't know where their father had gone. But Rudy had a hunch where he could find the old footballer.

CHAPTER 13

Rudy drove to Burned Out Park and parked in one of his usual spaces. The place was absolutely deserted, which surprised him very little—he thought of it as one of the ugliest parks he had ever been to, even on the sunniest, most glorious days, few people visited it, mainly because Claymore had better parks with more trees. Looking up and around, he observed, for the first time, how poorly lit the parking lot was. He hoped there was no crazy guy with a gun hiding in the darkness.

He got out of his Passat and entered the park, mostly groping his way along till he reached the part where he and Mitch usually played. *Great place for a murder*, he thought, shivering in the evening heat.

"Mitch!" he called out. "You there, guy?"

"Who wants to know?" a voice called back.

"It's Rudy."

"Hoss? For real?"

Rudy thought Mitch's voice seemed to be floating in the air. He squinted around some more, managed to orient himself and figured out that Mitch was sitting on the bronze horse, two dozen feet above those on the ground.

The boy began climbing to join the man, cursing the darkness that prevented him from seeing where he was. Soon he could sort of make out Mitch's form, which appeared to be reclining on the horse, relaxing and enjoying himself just fine in the middle of the night as his children, blocks away, tried to figure out where he was and if he was still alive.

"Mitch," he said, panting, "do you know what time it is? Do you know where you are? What's the big idea?"

"How come you're late? Go get the ball," Mitch replied.

Rudy closed his eyes and took a deep breath. "No football right now, guy. Go home. It's late. Come on, I'll drive you."

"Did my dad send you to get me?"

"Huh?" Then, "Mitch, what is your age?"

"You *know* my age."

"Can't remember. Tell me again."

"Same age as you, Hoss. Stop jerkin' me around."

Rudy sat at the base of the statue, under the horse, and the two of them stayed silent for a few minutes. How many hours had he spent with Mitch at this park, wondering why a retired Raider apparently had nothing better to do than throw or kick a football around with a teenager? Rudy now knew the answer: Because Mitch thought he, too, was a teenager.

How could it be? Surely Mitch knew about his own distinguished past in the NFL, although he didn't mention it, and when Rudy did, Mitch said very little about it, as if it bored him. The only thing he seemed to have any use for was football.

Rudy looked into the darkness of the night and thought for a few moments about how to resume their conversation. Finally he said, "Your kids are Mario and Kimberley. You know who they are, right?"

"Duh."

"Well, they're very worried about you. How about we get into my car so I can drive you home?"

"OK."

When they got into Rudy's Passat, Mitch grinned.. "This is a nice ride you got here, Hoss. I bet when you go cruising for chicks, you make out pretty good."

I wish. "So, Mitch, where are we going?"

"My place."

"Where's that?"

"Oh, you know the way."

"No, sir. You'll have to tell me."

"Just down the road some."

As they passed the exterminator's store, Rudy said, "Remember when we poured sugar into that guy's place?"

Mitch cackled. "That's a great idea! We should do it sometime. I hate that guy. I always have."

"Oh." They drove around, and Mitch said stuff like, "Problem with Claymore is that it's just getting too big. Before long, it's gonna look like Los Angeles."

Rudy rolled his eyes. Then he heard barking and saw, in the headlights, a big black poodle.

"Hey, Pierre!" Mitch yelled at the dog. "You shouldn't run out into the street like that! You could've been killed!"

"Dad!" Kimberley came running out into the street. "I'm so glad you're home! We were about to call the cops."

Mitch got out of the car, Kimberley hugged him and Rudy thought, *No need to thank me. Next time he forgets who he is and where he lives, just call me. I'll drop everything and come running.*

"You're a good boy, Pierre," said Mitch, patting the dog on the head.

"She's a *girl*, Dad," said Kimberley. "Her name in Trina."

Missus Cruncietti came out and hugged her husband. "Kimberley, call Mario on his cell and tell him Dad's back." To Rudy she said, "Thanks for your help."

He nodded and drove off, thinking that was the first time any of Mitch's people had been polite to him.

At three in the morning, Rudy sat in his bedroom, entering dozens of words into his MacBook Pro. Although he'd had a long and weird night, he could not sleep; Mitch's behavior had disturbed him so much that he could not get any shuteye until he'd gotten some answers about Captain Crunch, and he knew perfectly well that he couldn't just go up to Mario or Kimberley and say, "What's the deal with your old man, anyway?"

Some of the results he got suggested that Mitch might be senile, but Rudy rejected that immediately. Senility happened to old folks; Mitch was still in late middle age. But if Mitch didn't yet suffer from senility, he definitely had had enough head injuries—concussions—to compromise his mental faculties. Rudy went to iTunes and listened to podcasts. He heard a neurologist say, "Even when football players bump helmets to increase morale, they're giving each other concussions. A small concussion is still a concussion." The doctor went on to say that head injuries could destroy people's minds in peculiar ways: A person could forget what he had to eat an hour ago yet clearly remember experiences from decades earlier.

Like a retired jock I know who thinks he's still in adolescence.

Rudy shut off his MacBook Pro and sat back. Now he understood much more about Mitch's bizarre behavior and why his kids copped such attitudes whenever anyone mentioned him. Rudy now knew why the storekeepers waved him on past without expecting to be paid—they knew his wife would come by soon to settle up with them. As a local hero—a tall, muscular man, a former Raider with two Super Bowl rings to boast of—Mitch was cut more than his share of slack by the good folks of Claymore, who indulged him as they might a precocious, accomplished child given to extreme, highly provocative behavior. None of them really had clue that in reality he was a very sick man.

Rudy sighed. He swallowed hard and felt tears sting his eyes. He liked to think he was a rough-and-tumble guy who didn't let others' problems become his own. But the truth was, he was an empathic young man who hated to see other people suffer. The Internet sites said that Alzheimer's victims just got worse and worse. For the time being, Mitch's family had his back, but that situation wouldn't last forever. At some point, Mitch's mind would be reduced to mush. What would happen to him and his family then?

On Sunday, Rudy sat on his bed, nodding off as he read through the Pioneers' playbook. He heard tapping on his window and got up to see what who was there.

Nobody was tapping; someone was throwing pebbles at his window. He smiled when he saw who it was.

"Lauren, why don't you just knock on my door?"

"Because," she retorted, "throwing pebbles at windows is more fun."

"Meet me at my front door."

She did as told, and he let her in.

"I wasn't sure if your mom would be here," Lauren said. "I don't know if she totally approves of me yet."

"She's out there somewhere, taking pictures of Claymore's natural wonders so she can post them online."

"So she's not here? That's rad." Lauren leaned over and kissed him. He felt her lips on his but did not make much of an effort to kiss back.

She ended their kiss and eyeballed him. "You mad at me or something?"

"Nope. But maybe I should be. That party last night? One dude tried to whack me with a golf club and a couple of others wanted to punch me out."

She put her hands on her hips. "That was all a misunderstanding. Plus, they were drunk. Everything's OK now."

Rudy shook his head. "Negative. There was a huge amount of bad energy in that house. Those guys wanted to kick my butt—"

"But they *didn't* kick your butt." She stepped around him and looked at his backside. "Your butt definitely looks unkicked. Nice buns, by the way."

Rudy laughed in spite of himself. "Well, I do have to admit I find you attractive."

"Everybody does. It's not being irresistible. You might say it's my burden to bear."

"You poor thing."

"Anyway, I don't want all those guys who want me. I want you."

"Everyone around here thinks you're Mario's girl. You probably keep forgetting that."

Lauren made a face. "Well, gee, if Mario and I are a couple, *he* seems to forget that I'm his and he's mine. He certainly pays plenty of attention to all the chicks who throw themselves at him."

"Shame on him."

She pouted. "I don't like this arrangement the way it is. Couldn't you and I despise each other and still suck face?"

"We don't despise each other. You're the only friend I have in this town."

"Does that mean we can suck face?"

Just then they heard the wail of a police siren. They watched as the cruiser pulled up to Rudy's driveway.

"Isn't that Michaelson?" asked Lauren. "Doesn't he have anything better to do than hassle you?"

"I have a feeling my Sunday is going to suck."

"Rudy," said Officer Michaelson as the two sat in the police station, "I'm going to tell you something you already know: This can be as easy or as difficult as you want it to be."

"I hear you. The thing is, I am innocent."

"I believe you. Problem is, I think you know you toilet-papered the exterminator's store. If you don't tell me that person's name, I'm going to have to book you and press charges. Don't want to, but that's just how the law works."

"Then the law sucks," Rudy said.

"Is that all you have to say?"

"I can't believe you're going to bust me over putting toilet paper on someone's building. Especially when I didn't do it."

"Well, you can walk away from this thing by telling me who did it. The way it is now, because of your, uh, history with Elmer the Exterminator, you're our main suspect, and he wants to press charges. He has every right to do that, and we have every obligation to put you through the juvenile-justice system. But, as I say, you can walk away from this ugliness by telling me what you know."

Rudy knew very little about diminished-capacity law, but it was a no-brainer that Mitch would skate as soon as a shrink checked him out and saw what sorry shape the poor guy was in.

Still and all, Rudy thought, *why should I be a snitch? Mitch was my friend when no one else had any use for me.* The Cruncietti family seemed bent on hiding Captain Crunch's condition from the world for as long as possible. If this toilet-paper stunt went to trial and the true culprit's identity became known, that family would feel humiliated. Rudy didn't much care about Mario and Kimberley's dignity because they had seemed pretty indifferent to his, but Rudy felt badly about Mitch, whose mental state would deteriorate drastically in the months ahead. Mitch had shown him some kindness and friendship, and the younger guy wasn't the type to forget such favors.

"No comment," he said to Officer Bruce Michaelson.

The cop sighed and closed his eyes. "You have the right to remain silent…"

Rudy's mom was less understanding this time around. She had gotten into her SUV and driven miles into the Inland Valley in search of natural beauty to photograph. As she stood in the middle of nowhere, her cell phone had started ringing. When she pressed it to her ear, Kathleen Maxa heard Bruce Michaelson going on and on about how she should return to Claymore immediately and get her son out of jail.

When she finally made it back home, she marched into the police station, wiping sweat from her face, and exclaimed, "Rudy! You've been busted! I can't believe this is happening! You have a police record now, did you know that? Who are you protecting, anyway? Your bimbo girlfriend?"

"No girlfriend here," Rudy said. "The chicks here don't like me. They call me Cracker, Okie and Hoosier, among other things. I'm going to become a professional virgin."

"Why can't you get along here? Back in Indy, you led a reasonably normal life. Why can't you do that here?"

He shrugged. "I'm trying. I don't go looking for trouble. It goes looking for me, and it finds me."

Officer Bruce Michaelson came in with a cup of hot coffee and a couple of glazed donuts. "Sorry if the donuts aren't too fresh," he said with a sheepish smile. Rudy could tell that the cop had a big crush on his mom. He hoped she wouldn't marry the guy; having a cop for a stepdad would be pretty lame.

Kathleen Maxa looked up at the man with a strained smile. "You've been wonderful, Bruce. I'm really sorry about all this. I guarantee you that back in Indiana Rudy did *not* get into trouble."

The cop nodded. "Spend more time with him. Talk to him. I don't think you've got a Charles Manson or Richard Ramirez here, but as long as he shuts up and refuses to cooperate with the police, the more trouble he'll be in."

The ragging continued as the two Maxas left the police station and climbed into Kathleen's SUV.

"Rudy," she said, blasting the air conditioner so that it would be colder than winter inside the vehicle, just the way they both liked it, "you've got to help me to help you. Do you think I want to become the laughingstock of Claymore because of my acting-out son? It seems that every time I turn around, you're back at the police station and I'm getting a call to come and get you. I don't want to have to be as pushy and tyrannical as your father..." She shuddered. "I hate the thought of getting him on the phone and telling him about what's been happening here."

"Then *I'll* tell him about it." Rudy was totally at ease with the idea of calling Gordy "Boss Daddy" Maxa and telling him about these scrapes with the Claymore cops. He didn't like the idea of letting his mother get on the phone to Boss Daddy, who would bellow at her for an hour about what an unfit mother Rudy had. Mom had already put up with enough of Boss Daddy's temper tantrums to last a dozen millennia.

She cackled. "*You're* going to call him? I'd love to see that."

"I'll do it. I'll call him and tell him what's going on."

"Better start with me. I would *love* to know what's going on."

He said nothing. He could think of nothing to say to her, and he felt very disappointed in himself. Whether or not either of them cared to admit it, each was the only one the other had. Divorced mother and only child, both runaways from the House of Boss Daddy. She had always been her son's confidante, someone he could always be himself around, but now he was starting to shut her out of his life.

They drove in silence to her workplace, the news service. He sat just outside her office as she uploaded the images she'd just taken in the Inland Valley. He felt as if he were still a small child and his mother had said, "I don't trust you to be at home by yourself, so you can just sit there outside my office, so I can keep an eye on you."

He sat low in the chair, listening with surly muteness as his mother clicked and typed away on her computer, gathering the names and phone numbers of Claymore attorneys who practiced juvie law. He eyeballed the many images on the wall a few feet away. At the top it said HISTORY OF CLAYMORE. Rudy rested his eyes for a few minutes on a picture he recognized right away as Burned Out Park, which looked as boring in that image as it did in real life. He spotted another photo, this one of the exterminator's store, but the huge spider wasn't there, although a nasty, winkled, skinny man was. The sign said

DUFUS HARDWARE.

Rudy thought for a few minutes. Elmer's store, in the 1970s, had been Dufus Hardware. Mitch kept calling Elmer "Doofus," when he meant Dufus, the former proprietor of the store he and Rudy vandalized. Rudy wondered why Mitch kept calling him "Hoss," the name of the character from the old Western TV show. American men sometimes called each other Hoss in a very casual way, but Rudy wondered if there might have been someone by that name in Mitch's life at some point and he had that person confused with this new kid in town.

Rudy was sick of it all: Claymore, the high school and football team, Officer Bruce Michaelson and, most of all, Mitch Cruncietti. He closed his eyes and for the longest time tried very hard to think of nothing at all.

CHAPTER 14

Rudy arrived at Claymore High just in time to see a girl in a baseball slip a note into his locker.

"Lauren," he said, "how many times I gotta tell you? You got something to say, say it to my face. Don't be writing it down and slipping it into my locker. Besides, what if Super Mario saw it?"

The girl turned around. "I'm not Lauren," she said. "I'm Kimberley Cruncietti."

"Oh." Rudy swallowed as he took in the sight of her and realized how well she filled out her Levi's and sweatshirt. In the brief time he had known her, he hadn't thought of her as an ugly girl, just a girl with an ugly attitude.

"I put a note in there," she said, tapping on his locker door. "The note says, 'How come you knew where to find my dad when nobody else did?'"

Rudy frowned. He wanted to tell her it was none of her business. Instead, he told her about his first days in Claymore and how he had gone to Burned Out Park to train alone. Mitch had invited himself to be Rudy's playmate. As he stood there and told Kimberley these things, he knew he had every right to say them, but at the same time he felt he was telling her things that were none of her business. He thought they were none of *his* business, too. "He has Alzheimer's, you know. I've read about it online. It's fairly common for NFL guys to get it because of all the head injuries."

Kimberley blanched. "We've tried so hard to keep it a secret," she muttered.

"I won't tell anyone," Rudy said.

Kimberley thrust out her chin. "You sound like it's something we should be *ashamed* of. It's a private family matter, and we're dealing with it the best we can."

"You should be proud of him. Know what my father does for a living? He's a car salesman in Terre Haute, Indiana. He cares more about those cars and his customers than he does his family. If my dad had played for the Raiders, I would be bragging about it all the time. When I first moved out here, I thought I knew everything about football, but Mitch has taught me more than anyone in the past few months."

She snarled. "You're a fool. You've hung out with my dad and figured out that he's mentally impaired from head injuries, and you still want to play football."

"Mario plays football, too."

"Yeah, and he's a fool, too. He looks at our dad and says, 'Well, that will never happen to *me*.' Wanna bet?"

Rudy nodded. "I understand."

Kimberley shook her head. "You understand nothing. You suit up and play football and think you're invincible. Well, you're not."

"I've never said I was. Anyway, when my folks called it quits, it had a huge impact on me, so I know that your dad's medical problems affect your whole family. And that's too bad." He added, "Sorry that I mistook you for Lauren a minute ago."

"Don't apologize. It's the ultimate compliment. Unfortunately."

"Why do you dislike her?"

"Because I know her. She's dated my brother on and off for quite a while. She's bad news."

"So maybe I should stay away from her."

"Good idea."

Rudy thought for a moment. "What's it to you if I get friendly with Lauren and she breaks my heart? You don't seem to have much use for me."

"Well, you brought my dad home. You did us a big favor. Maybe you're not so bad after all."

"No big deal. You guys were, like, 'Dad's not home. We don't know where he's gone.' I was, like, 'Oh, I think I can guess where he is.'"

"But it *was* a big deal to us. The fact is, we had a problem—our problem, not yours—and you basically said. 'I can help you with your problem.' You were under no obligation to help us, but you cared enough to do it. Do you think Lauren cares about anything expect having everyone kiss her butt and say, 'Girlfriend, you are just too awesome!'?"

Rudy nodded. "She needs to expand her horizons."

Kimberley chuckled. "That," she said, "is an understatement."

Coach Hartman sat back and said, "Maxa, I'll give you an A-plus for effort. You block as well as any boy I've ever coached. If you could go to Gold's Gym five times per week and beef up by thirty pounds, you could get a college scholarship as a linebacker."

"I'd rather be a quarterback—"

Hartman waved him off. "This conversation isn't about you. It's about Cruncietti. I'm concerned about him."

He's afraid of being hit, Coach. Simple as that. Quarterback who's afraid of being hit isn't of much use to anyone. "Not sure what you're talking about."

Hartman frowned. "He's lost his edge. When you get ready to take the snap, you can't have any fear. All you should be thinking about is each play and advancing that football. But once you've lost that fearlessness, well, it's time to hang up your cleats and sell insurance because your football days are over. I suppose you understand that."

Rudy nodded. "I hear ya." Getting his shot at QB turned him on, and taking it away from Super Mario? Well, that would be a very nice bonus.

Hartman eyeballed him. "I think you and I know why all this is happening, don't we?"

Rudy shrugged. "Explain it to me."

"Ever since you got here from Indiana, you've been after his job on the football team. The thing is, you're a pretty competent quarterback and he knows it. So you two fellas aren't exactly friends. Well, there's no law against rivalries, but your presence around here stresses him out. Also, there's this matter of you and Lauren Hutsch. Two fellas liking the same girl. Don't sit there and pretend you don't know what I'm talking about."

Rudy gulped. "Don't take this the wrong way, but my love life is none of your business."

"You're right. Just find a different chick to cruise,

all right?"

"Excuse me?"

"You need to remember that you're the new guy here. Mario Cruncietti? He led the Pioneers to a perfect season last year, so he's earned his spot as quarterback until I'm convinced that he can't get the job done any longer." Then, "You see, Maxa, Claymore is a pretty boring place in many ways, so the folks here get excited over the few things here that are worth getting excited about, and one of those things is the Pioneers. When they win, everyone gives the credit to the players; when they lose, folks blame me. They say, 'What's your problem, Coach?' Fortunately, they haven't lost in a long time. If they started losing, I would lose my job, and I very much want to keep my job. Here's the bottom line: I keep from sticking my nose into my players' personal business until their personal business messes up their heads to the point where they may be unable to win football games for me."

Presently Rudy left Hartman's office, shaking his head at the coach's logic: Win, win, win. Didn't the old dude know there was more to life than football games?

It's all good, he said to himself. *You were trying to cut Lauren loose, anyway, so do as he says and find other chicks to cruise.*

Still, he resented the fact that he had gone into the coach's office to be told, "Maxa, I don't like all the attention you and Lauren have paid to each other. Go cruise another chick," and Rudy had replied, "Yessir, I'll do that."

The coach's office was located at the end of a hallway whose walls were lined with trophies and whatnot that Claymore High's sports teams had won over the years. Rudy noticed one in particular, a large, shiny brass plaque. It said:

MITCHELL CRUNCIETTI
CLASS OF 1973
Second Round Draft Pick
Oakland Raiders, 1977

Rudy found the 1973 team picture. Mitch stood there, tall and smiling, buff and cut. But then Rudy started looking for someone else—the guy named Hoss. If Mitch seemed to be living mentally in adolescence, Hoss was probably one of his Claymore High pals who played on the '73 Pioneers.

Naturally, the faces on the wall meant zilch to Rudy. He searched among the names for someone named Hoss.

He found no one by that name, but the beefy kid next to Mitch was named Michael Hossman. Could *he* be "Hoss"?

Rudy cringed every time he thought of his hearing date—December 10. On that day, he would put on a suit and stand before a judge and tell the man or woman in the black robe why he had gone to Elmer the Exterminator and put toilet paper all over the front of the store. If he pleaded not guilty, he would need to tell the judge who had actually done it.

"Those are your options, Rudy," said the discount lawyer his mother had hired for him. "My advice? If you're innocent and know who did it, say so. Spare yourself some grief."

The lawyer, a fat, balding guy with a funny accent, didn't have the greatest bedside manner, but Rudy had to admit that he made sense. It would do no good for Rudy to say to the judge, "I didn't do it but I know who did. Unfortunately, I can't tell you his name. Can't we just forget about this whole incident?"

Or:

"The truth is that a middle-aged Alzheimer's victim, a retired Raider named Mitch Cruncietti, toilet-papered the front of a store whose former proprietor, long since retired and probably dead by now, had been nasty to the former footballer. This same man seemed to think that the accused, one Rudy Maxa—me—is his childhood pal Michael Hossman."

Would the judge believe *that*, either?

Rudy decided that the best idea would be to speak to Michael Hossman. If he could find the man, of course.

In the Inland Valley white pages, Rudy found two Hossmans, neither of whom was Michael. The first was an old lady who ragged on Rudy about how many people called her each day wanting something, usually money. The second person, a guy, kept their conversation brief.

"Yeah, I've heard there are some other Hossmans out here, but I've never bothered to check them out and they've never bothered with me." Click.

Rudy surfed the Internet some more and learned

that there were vast numbers of Hossmans scattered across the continent. Which, if any, was the M. Hossman he sought? He really had no idea, since he was just a high-school kid, not a private dick.

He slumped back in chair and let out a huge sigh of frustration. Just as he was about to turn off his computer and give it a miss for the day, he saw a terse message on his screen:

FIND WHO YOU'RE LOOKING FOR.
NOW.
FREE.

He had seen such come-ons before, of course. Mostly the site delivered immediate results, but the "free" part was a bit trickier; they wanted the user's credit-card number first. If it was free, Rudy wondered, how come they needed payment info?

Well, this site seemed the real deal—no gimmicks, no American Express number needed, just do your search, get whatever you need and that was all. Rudy chuckled at the notion of sitting down over a few bottles of Coors with Mario two decades from now, their boyhood rivalries reduced to the most trivial of jokes. Lauren, now a farmer's wife, fat and earthy, mother of six. A small-town beauty who'd gone to Hollywood for five years to make millions and win Oscars but instead ended up dancing nude in West Hollywood nightclubs.

He followed the instructions and filled out the online form. In the box where it said ANY ADDITIONAL INFORMATION, he wrote:

We played football together in Burned Out Park and for the

Claymore High School Pioneers. In our free time, we made life difficult for an old storekeeper named Dufus. Where are you, Hoss?

Mitch C.

The last action was to press the SUBMIT button. He thought for a moment. Was it legal for him to pretend to be Mitch Cruncietti online? And what about sending a message to Mike Hossman and signing it as Mitch? Could Rudy get into a crapload of trouble for this stunt? He didn't think so. He couldn't feature Mitch visiting this Website and finding that where-are-you? message Rudy had written Hoss. Many times, Mitch struck Rudy as being so totally confused that the old guy probably would not recognize his own driver's license.

Rudy pressed the SUBMIT button and hoped for the best.

CHAPTER 16

The Claymore Pioneers kept winning football games despite tentative performances from Mario Cruncietti. The quarterback's problems were too subtle for anyone in the stands to perceive—he left the pocket a moment or two too soon, he seemed in a hurry to throw the pass, he ran away after handing off the ball as if being chased down the street by bullies. Rudy could also see the frowns and pursed lips of Coach Hartman and Lauren.

Rudy wondered if Mario knew just how jittery he was, but it seemed to make little difference; as soon as the quarterback took the snap, Rudy slammed into his defender as Mario handed off to Joey Rossi, who ran like a bull dog through the spacious hole Rudy had just created. All day, Rudy marveled at how Mitch's advice—"Take on your opponent with your shoulder, hit him just so and watch him drop to his knees"—worked so well so often. Rudy craved the same intense contact that Mario so desperately avoided.

The Pioneers were having so much success, and receiving such adulation, that even Rudy got some pats on his back for his fierce blocking that ripped open gaping holes for Joey. But Claymore was a small town full of big mouths; Rudy figured out fast that people were jawing about his upcoming court date to face criminal charges (yes); they said he'd had to punch his way out of Grant Miller's party (no); he drove a stolen car (partly yes; he's pilfered it from his father); he'd stolen Mario Cruncietti squeeze and then cut her loose (mostly no); he and Lauren had publicly ended their relationship but were making out in secret (no, but Rudy wished it were so).

Rudy said to himself, *Pay no attention—what they say means nothing.* But the truth was, he paid much attention to them and cared a great deal about their opinions of him. He felt gratified by the admiring faces he encountered and the warmth in their voices as they greeted him.

"Rudy," Lauren said, "you are in style now. You are so hot that we could fry and egg on your buns and call it a breakfast sandwich! And I checked you out first! Yea, me!"

He would enjoyed her rap much more if she hadn't done it so loudly, and within earshot so many others who would certainly pass it on to Mario. Yet her gushing felt as fine to him as the sweetest cologne, and he easily convinced himself that her interest in him was genuine and the two of them could become a very serious item.

The problem, if one could call it that, was simple: Lauren the Football Groupie understood Rudy's job. He knocked guys to their knees so that big holes opened up and Joey could carry the football for many yards or even into the end zone. Put another way, Rudy had the guts while Joey got the glory.

The new kid in town had been putting others' interests before his own. He reminded himself to borrow a copy of *Looking Out for #1* the next time he went to the school library.

At home that day, Rudy opened his MacBook Pro and went online. He checked his emails and, with a big hard swallow, opened one that said:

For real? Is that you, Mitch G.?

My name is Theresa Valente. We had a few classes together. I work for the state government here in Sacramento, where so many of us from Claymore High seemed to have ended up. Civil service work is often boring but pays moderately well.

If you didn't know, we Claymore High alumni in Sacramento have our own little club here and we meet once per month for drinks as we get reacquainted. Nostalgia is fun; as the old saying goes, "The older I get, the better I was"! The reason I'm writing is to invite you to join us' Sacramento isn't that far form Claymore, and since we were all so thrilled when you turned pro and played for the Raiders for all those years, we think it would be terrific to see you again!

Looking forward to seeing you,

Theresa V.

Rudy snarled. Not Hoss! Nuts! Just some woman in Sacramento who wanted Mitch to drive out there for cocktails and gossip. But what were the odds that Rudy's message would be read—and replied to—by Hoss? The Internet was a vast place, so Rudy told himself he should feel lucky that someone did reply to his message. Then he thought: *If this Theresa person knows me, and she makes a point of staying in touch with the other Claymore High people from her class, maybe she knows how I can contact Hoss.*

He wrote back to Theresa:

Theresa,

Terrific to hear from a Claymore alumna! The monthly reunions sound like fun; maybe I'll get to Sacramento soon and join you. BTW, do you know anything about Michael Hossman? Any current contact into would be very much appreciated. Who knows? Maybe Hoss could be my date for the next reunion in Sacramento!

Rudy signed it "Mitch," and a little voice in his head said, *Missus Maxa, would you look what your son Rudy is doing?*

Theresa got back to him within an hour. He had a hunch she had been hot for Mitch when they were classmates. He assumed that many girls back then wanted to date big, handsome Mitch.

Her email this time contained endless boring crap about how big and crowded Sacramento had become. She said she had married a doctor and had three delightful children. Ho hum, Rudy thought until he got to the bottom paragraph:

Unfortunately, we haven't heard very much from Hoss. It's so sad how we were friends as kids, but then we grew up and went in different directions. I do have an address **for him—85 Frankie Lane**, **Yardbird, California—that I believe is fairly current.**

Rudy brightened up a bit. He and his mom had covered enough of northern California in her SUV for him to know that Yardbird wasn't terribly far away, about half an hour from Claymore, depending on how fast he dogged out his VW and how many California Highway Patrol officers were on duty that day to pull him over for tickets.

CHAPTER 17

Rudy pulled up to 85 Frankie Lane to discover that it was not a house but an old brick warehouse or factory that developers had turned into a fancy mall of sorts, with offices upstairs.

Rudy parked his car and went inside. Yardbird didn't strike him as the kind of place that California tourism brochures urged as a "place to go while in the Golden State"—neither did Claymore, in fact—but this old brick building had been restored into something fresh and handsome, and he saw plenty of sun-kissed shoppers entering and exiting the stores. Was this really Hoss' address? If so, where could he be?

The answer was on the building's directory:

202—Hossman, Michael, Attorney-at-Law

No, Hoss didn't live here. He practiced law here.

Rudy climbed the stairs, wondering how the next fifteen minutes would go. He was about to meet the man Mitch thought he was. *This is all just too weird,* was Rudy's main thought. His second thought was, *I like weird.*

As he stood at the closed door that bore the number 202, he felt for a moment the desire to run, to get back into his Passat and head back to Claymore and forget about this lunacy. Then he grabbed the doorknob, turned it and opened the door.

The receptionist looked up at him and smiled.

"May I help you?"

"Is Mister Hossman available?"

"Yes. Do you have an appointment?"

"No, ma'am. I'm here on a personal matter."

She frowned. "Which is…?"

Rudy squirmed. "We have a mutual friend."

"Who's our friend?" asked a deep male voice from another part of the room.

Rudy looked in his direction. The man, in his shirtsleeves, stood tall, burly and balding.

"Mitch Cruncietti."

The man laughed. "There's a name I haven't heard in a few years. How do you know him?"

"We're neighbors. He helps me with football."

"Then come into my office and you can update me on Mitch."

Rudy nodded and the two sat in the lawyer's office.

"Mister Hossman—"

The man held up a hand. "Hoss. Everyone calls me that now. Mitch started that a million years ago." He shook his head and laughed. "We were such bad boys back then."

Rudy smirked. "I'll bet Dufus the storekeeper thought so, too."

Hoss laughed some more. "That old coot owned one of the local stores, but he thought he was the mayor of Claymore! I think he even wanted to run for that office at some point. If he even saw Mitch and me on the street, he would call the cops. If there were kids smoking pot in Burned Out Park, he would call the cops, and the cops would say, 'Well, what do you want us to do about it?' I think the old guy went out to confront the dopers and he tried to make a citizen's arrest. I suppose Mitch has told you all about that."

"Well, that's why I'm here. Mitch is still at war with Dufus."

Hoss frowned. "What do you mean? Dufus died years ago."

Rudy nodded. "Well, for the past while, Dufus' old store has been an extermination service. But Mitch thinks the exterminator is Dufus. He thinks he's still a teenager. He thinks I'm his pal Hoss."

Hoss sat there, face expressionless, brain gathering the facts, sorting them out. "Why does he think that?"

"Because," Rudy said, "he has Alzheimer's disease."

Hoss eyeballed him. "I thought only old folks got that."

"Well, it's different in Mitch's case. It's the early-onset kind, and the experts think it has to do with all the head injuries, large and small, that happen during football games."

Hoss pursed his lips. "I've heard about that, but I didn't think it was the same kind of mental deterioration that old folks have." He looked down and grinned. "Back when I knew him, Mitch was capable of pretty peculiar behavior. I don't think he's ever been what other people might call 'normal.' Maybe that's why he was so much fun to hang out with." Then his face darkened. "How severely impaired *is* he?"

"Oh, if you spend just a few minutes around him, he seems as normal as the next guy. But after a while, you'd start to notice that he thinks he's still a teenager even though he understands that he is married with children. I don't know just how much of his life he comprehends—maybe sometimes he's pretending he doesn't understand just so he can see people's reaction. He does seem to understand Burned Out Park, football and this guy named Hoss. That's how we met—I was at the park, minding my own business, when along came Mitch. He was, like, 'Hey, Hoss! I see you got a football! Let's play!'"

"Burned Out Park," Hoss murmured, smirking. "That ugly place was like a second home to us— literally. When we weren't playing catch there, we went out carousing and chasing girls. Our parents both said, 'We won't be having you staggering home with liquor on your breath, so if you're drunk, you'll have to sleep somewhere else.' Mitch and I slept on Burned Out Park benches on those nights. I still don't know how we survived that period.

"I used to watch Mitch when he played for the Raiders, and let me tell you, he really lived up to the black-and-silver's reputation for being the bad boys of the NFL. He could hit just as hard as any guy in the league, and sometimes I think the Raiders' opponents were afraid of him. Can you imagine that?"

"It sounds like you two were very tight when you were kids. How come you lost touch with each other?"

"The same thing that brought us together— football. Even in high school, he was a pro prospect but I wasn't. He had the killer instinct, or the edge, or whatever you want to call it, but I didn't. So we just went our separate ways. Had nothing to say to each other."

Just the telephone rang, and Hoss told his receptionist to take a message. To Rudy he said, "I'm sorry to hear about Mitch's problems, and I don't want to sound rude, but what's it to me? Sounds like he needs a neurologist, not a lawyer."

Rudy felt his face redden as he said, "Mitch has a problem that has sort of become my problem, too. He's at war with Elmer the Exterminator because he thinks Elmer is Dufus, the old guy who had the store when he and you were kids. Mitch has been playing practical jokes on Elmer, but you know Mitch—he doesn't know when to quit. Anyway, the Claymore cops have decided I'm the guilty party, and now I have a court date, and the only way I can defend myself is by pointing my finger at Mitch and saying, 'See this poor guy with Alzheimer's? He's your man!'"

"Sounds like small-time stuff. Nobody has been killed or injured—just some vandalism. Mitch just needs to make it clear to the court that he's not responsible for his actions due to his medical condition. Easy enough to do."

"Bad deal," Rudy said, shaking his head. "That means I would have to snitch him off, and I hate snitches. Then I'll have to say to the world, 'Mitch Cruncietti is losing his marbles due to Alzheimer's.'"

Hoss smiled. "You can't take on all of this as your personal burden to bear. You've done nothing to Elmer the Exterminator, so you shouldn't be punished. Actually, you'd be doing Mitch a favor by disclosing his illness. People get sick, Rudy. They get old, get sick and die. That's just how life is.

Alzheimer's is a disease, not a crime."

Rudy shrugged. "I guess. But it sounds too weird. I mean, can I really go into court and say, 'Mitch is living decades in the past and thinks I'm his old pal Hoss'?"

The lawyer chuckled. "Stranger things have been spoken and heard in court, I can assure you. It sounds to me like what you need is for me to say, 'Yes, it's true what Rudy says about Mitch's old life when he and I were friends.' Is that about right?"

"Yessir." Then, "I find all of this totally embarrassing. It's a funny thing, you know. When I was at Burned Out Park with Mitch? It was like I was Hoss—he made me Hoss—and I felt completely comfortable in that role. There was never any awkwardness—it was like we had known each other all our lives. My mom and I moved here from Indiana in late August and it turns out he's *still* the only friend I have in Claymore. Can you believe it?"

"Yes, I can. Mitch has always had charisma. Back in Claymore High, all the guys wanted to know him and all the chicks wanted to date him."

Rudy sighed and looked at the floor. "I don't like any of this. As I said, he's about the only friend I have in Claymore. The other people don't seem to have much use for me."

Hoss handed Rudy a business card. "If the cops start giving you a hard time, have them contact me. Yardbird isn't that far from Claymore. I'll be happy to tell them what's going on."

Rudy smiled as he shook Hoss' hand. "I sure appreciate that. From the way Mitch treats me and calls me Hoss...well, I knew that the real Hoss would be a stand-up guy."

As they walked to the door, Hoss said, "It's odd that you should come and see me right now. I'd mostly forgotten about Mitch, but then just a little while ago I heard about his election into the hall of fame—"

Rudy's face lit up. "I'm from Indy! Canton, Ohio, isn't that far away! I've been to the Hall of Fame! It's so rad—"

"Not *that* hall of fame, the Inland Valley College one." Hoss laughed. "Mitch had a good run with the Raiders, but he wasn't Lawrence Taylor or Dick Butkus. Still, they want to enshrine him at our high school, and I think that's a great idea."

"For sure!"

"Only thing is, will Mitch *understand* the honor he's receiving?"

"Yeah," Rudy said, "I think he will. The two things he can really wrap his brain around are football and his past. Plus, I'm sure he'll smile when he sees all those people cheering for him. He'll have a good time."

"As I say, I don't get back to Claymore very often—I'm swamped with work and other responsibilities here—and frankly, there's just nothing there for me any longer. But I'll make sure I go there to see Mitch on his induction day."

CHAPTER 18

The stands rocked and the air vibrated with the roar of football fans who had come out to see the Claymore High Pioneers get their butts kicked. The Gus Robertson Titans had the loudest, rowdiest home-field crowd Rudy had ever heard. He knew they wanted, *so* badly, to see their boys end the Pioneers' winning streak.

Coach Hartman bellowed at his offense, "Who called that timeout? Who did it? I'll rip his throat out! Anyone calls timeout, it's gonna be me!"

"I did it," replied Mario Cruncietti as he plopped onto the bench. "Guy butted me with his helmet. Where's the penalty flag? Where's the 'roughing the passer' call?"

"Negative," said the coach. "No foul on that play."

"Then how come my head hurts? How come my ears ring?"

"Mine are ringing, too," said Hartman. "It's that crowd. They're too noisy. They need to shut up."

"I saw him hit you," Rudy said to Mario. "It was legal."

"You're supposed to block for me," Mario

retorted. "You're supposed to protect me." Then, "I don't feel so good. I need to see a doctor."

The coach summoned Dr. Boyd, who was actually a dentist. He traveled with the team to all their road games and provided his services free of charge. As the dentist shone a light into the quarterback's eyes, Rudy watched their thirty seconds tick down to nothing.

"I'll go back in and do my best," said Mario.

"No," said the coach. "I'll use Lucido."

"What about *me*?" asked Rudy.

"You block. Now get your butt in there before the ref penalizes us for delay of game."

Rudy did just that, and on the next play, when a Titan charged at Lucido, Rudy rammed the kid so hard that his Titans helmet popped right off and bounced around on the turf like a severed head.

"Maxa," Coach Hartman said later, "I don't have to justify my decisions to you or anyone else. When I put in Lucido, everyone's thinking, 'Get Mario back in there—he's our star quarterback!' But when I put you in, they're thinking, 'Rudy's as good a quarterback as Mario; which one should have the job?' That's called *rivalry*, Maxa, and I don't want any part of it. You're a good quarterback—maybe too good."

The Pioneers managed to beat the Titans that evening by a touchdown. As the team whooped and hollered in jubilation, Hartman and Rudy snarled at each other. Nevertheless, they had another win to brag about, and their dream of going undefeated into eternity hadn't been crushed yet. The last team to beat them, the Epperson High Bandits, had done so with an overtime field goal so long ago that people kept forgetting when. But everyone knew that the Pioneers' next game, against the Bandits, would be their biggest challenge in quite some time.

Rudy saw Hartman's priorities much more clearly now. The coach, a diplomat, valued team harmony above all other things. Everyone could see that Mario's game had declined, but so what? Pretending that nothing was broken seemed better than fixing things. Besides, as long as Mario could hand off the ball to Rossi, and Rudy could rip open a hole or two for the running back, they would get into the end zone and win games. If Rudy the new kid didn't like it, well, that was just too bad.

The new kid no longer did any quarterbacking. He blocked like a fiend and, when playing cornerback, covered wide receivers like an old blanket. But he took no snaps, even during practice.

During drills, Hartman installed Rudy as cornerback and instructed him to blitz the quarterback—Mario. He nodded and eyeballed the Pioneers' stud, whose hands trembled as he looked this way and that before taking the snap.

Once he got the football, Mario cowered like a child as Rudy charged at him. But then the coach blew the play dead and Rudy, with some effort, threw himself past Mario and rolled on the ground before he got up. He would have loved to pound Mario, who had braced himself for the hit. But no—Rudy wouldn't let himself do it, no matter how much fun it would have been.

An hour later, as he stepped out of the shower, Rudy towel-dried his hair and heard a voice.

"Maxa."

He opened his eyes and saw Mario, snarling. Both boys wore only towels and everyone else had left. Would Mario pick a fight with him now? Rudy wondered. Back in Indy, his size and strength had scared off the bullies, who were mostly cowards afraid of getting into fights they weren't guaranteed to win.

"Congratulation," Rudy said. "I hear your dad is going into the Inland Valley College hall of fame."

Mario scowled. "What?"

"The Inland Valley College hall of fame. He's going in."

"Are you making fun of my father? Is that what you're doing?"

Rudy shook his head. "Not doin' anything of the kind."

"Ever since you moved here"—Mario took a deep breath and stuck out his chin—"you've tried to mess up my life. My father, my sister, my girlfriend—it's like you're our new hero just because you found my dad in the park and drove him home. Why don't you get a life, or go back to Ohio or wherever you came from and just leave us alone?"

The quarterback walked away, and Rudy just stood there for a few minutes, glad that neither of them had thrown any punches. He supposed he could take Mario if it came down to a fight, but fortunately that hadn't happened.

He also wondered why Mario didn't seem too happy about his father's induction into the hall of fame. Did Mario even know about that honor? Had Mitch told his family? Rudy then thought of something, and it made him sick to his stomach.

He made a point of seeing Kimberley at the beginning of school the next day, so he waited for her by her locker.

"Hey," he said.

She nodded hello. Kimberley had become friendlier towards him than Mario, which was to say that she didn't act like a black mamba whenever he came near.

"Kimberley," he said, "I need to ask you a question.

"Ask."

He paused. "Well, uh, when your dad gets stuff in the mail, does he read it?"

"Are you asking if he's illiterate? No, he's not. My father can read and write. He can fix his own breakfast, too. He can even wipe his own—"

"OK, I hear ya. I only asked because I know he's going to be inducted into the Inland Valley College hall of fame—"

"How do you know?" she asked frowning. "*I* didn't know that, and I'm his daughter. College hall of fame? That's kind of a big deal."

"It certainly is. See, they sent him a letter containing the good news. But considering his, uh, medical condition, I'm thinking there's a chance he threw away that litter without opening it or read it but didn't understand it. That's all I meant. No disrespect intended."

Kimberley eyeballed him. "Why," she asked, "do *we* seem to get all of *our* information about *our* father from *you*?"

Rudy blurted out a nervous laugh. "Well, in this case, I got the heads-up about the Inland Valley College thing from a guy who graduated at about the same time as Mitch. He's really psyched about this honor your dad's getting." Then, "I'm sorry if you or Mario thinks I'm trying to harass your family. I'm just trying to be your friend, and I wasn't sure if you knew about this hall of fame thing Mitch is going to receive."

Virginia Cruncietti sat at her MacBook Pro as her children stood behind her, watching as she clicked onto the Inland Valley College Website and smiled.

"That kid Rudy wasn't lying. Your dad is going into their hall of fame." She added, "How could we not know about this?"

Kimberley rolled her eyes. "You're kidding, right? I mean, it's *Dad* we're talking about. He can't keep anything straight."

"I've kept all those doctors' appointments," their mother said, her voice rising, "I've learned so much about Alzheimer's that they should give me a degree. And I know that Mitch Cruncietti would *not* forget something like being inducted to a hall of fame."

"He didn't forget," muttered Mario, "because he didn't learn it in the first place."

Kimberley made a face. "Have some respect. Don't speak about our dad that way."

Mario looked glum. "He's not our dad. He stopped being our dad once the Alzheimer's kicked in and stole him away from us."

"Maybe," Missus Cruncietti said, "the College forgot to send the letter, or got our address wrong…"

"Negative," said Mario. "I'm sure he got the letter. He probably made a paper airplane out of it and took it to Burned Out Park so he and Maxa could play with it."

"Your father *can* read. Your father *does* read," their mother said through gritted teeth.

122

"He *looks* at things," said Kimberley. "Not the same as reading."

Their mother got to her feet. "Let's go find that letter. Where does Dad keep his mail? In his study?"

Theirs was a five-bedroom house; they had converted the fifth bedroom into a study for Mitch. In it were a desk, reclining leather chair and bookshelves, all looking as if they had never been touched.

"Look at it," said the mother. "I ask you: Does this look like the den of someone whose mind is a mess?"

"It looks," replied Mario, "like the den of someone who doesn't even know he has a den."

They looked through the drawers and found only dust. "Well," Kimberley said, "now we've established that he doesn't use his den much, if at all. So we must ask ourselves: If he doesn't come in here, where does he go?"

"He goes," retorted Mario, "to Burned Out Park to play with his adopted son Rudy."

"Be serious," said Kimberley. "Where are his usual spots around here when he wants to be by himself? That's where he's usually going to check his mail."

"The porch," said the mother. "I get the mail, give him his and he goes to the porch."

"Seems to me," Mario told them, "that the porch swing out back seems jammed up."

The three Crunciettis hurried out to the swing and checked it out as if they were characters in *The Hurt Locker*, bomb specialists who suspected that the harmless-looking appliance might explode at any moment. Kimberley poked and prodded the inside of

123

the housing of the glider track. Then she reached in more deeply and pulled out a fistful of paper.

"Bingo," she muttered. "There's plenty more where this came from."

Missus Cruncietti choked back a sob.

"Lighten up, Ma," Mario said. "This is just more of the same. It's just the disease taking over."

She cleared her throat. "Every time something like this happens, it means we've lost a little bit more of him."

"You know what the doctors have told us," Kimberley said. "The meds help to a certain extent, but in the end Alzheimer's wins. We just have to deal with it."

"This"—Mario waved his arms around, indicating that his father had found a new place to stash his mail—"is not so bad. It's peculiar, but not so bad. It's not like he's dropping deuces into his pants and not knowing it."

Virginia Cruncietti nodded with a big sigh. For years she had been the premier realtor of burgeoning Claymore and one of the most envied businesspeople in the Inland Valley; now she depended upon her two children to advise her on the best way to cope with her ailing husband.

Kimberley did her best to smooth out some of her father's crumpled mail. "This one's from months ago. He's got them packed in there pretty tight."

"Let me go get a tool to open it up," Mario said. "Maybe Dad's put my birth certificate in with all the rest of the junk there."

He got a crowbar and opened up the box. Inside they discovered countless paper documents, wilted or discolored, all pressed together so that Mario had to pry them apart with much gentleness. He gathered together all of it, separated what was legible and disregarded the rest. The three of them sorted through the items that were still in decent shape.

Virginia Cruncietti said, "I think I understand now. He gets his mail, looks at it for a few seconds then puts it here, to look at later. But because he forgets everything, he never gets back to any of it and it just accumulates.

"Oh!" She held up a letter that looked somewhat less destroyed than the others. "This looks like something. It has the College logo." She read it aloud.

"'Dear Mister Cruncietti,

Congratulations and best wishes! We are pleased to inform you that we have elected you into the Inland Valley College Sports Hall of Fame.

"Your distinguished NFL career—including two Super Bowl rings!—has brought much gratification and satisfaction to our community. Your enshrinement in our Hall of Fame will make us as proud as it does you.

"We look forward to seeing you here for the ceremony on November 20...

"So he knew about it," muttered Missus Cruncietti.

"He knew about it for five minutes," said Mario. "Then he put it aside and forgot about it—and I do mean *forgot*."

"He's right, Mom," Kimberley said, staring at the ground. "That hall of fame ceremony hasn't happened yet. What are we going to do about it?"

Mario said, "Maybe we should go through all this mail and see if there's anything else here we should know about." Then, "Kimberley, are you thinking we should take Dad to that ceremony?"

She shrugged. "It's a big honor for Dad. He hasn't had much to be happy about lately. Maybe it would pick up his spirits."

Missus Cruncietti nodded. "It's an honor, and he certainly deserves it."

Mario shook his head. "Does he deserve to have us dress him up in his Sunday best and drive him out to the College so that everyone can see what a zombie he's become. Oh, yeah, that's a great idea. Everyone loves a good freak show."

Kimberley scowled. "Mario—!"

Mario scowled back. "Truth hurts, don't it? We could take him there and he wouldn't understand anything, and everyone would know it and gossip about him.."

"Do you really think that?" Kimberley retorted. "Or are you just bummed out because the ceremony falls on the same day as your next football game?"

"I'm just bummed out about Dad," Mario said, thin-lipped with anger. "Of course, you already knew that because you know me better than I know myself. Right? Well, if you think I'm full of crap, why don't you consult the big expert on him?"

"You mean the doctors?"

"No, I mean your *squeeze*. I mean, he's Dad's playmate, isn't he? He knows our old man better than we do."

"Since you brought it up, Rudy thinks Dad should go to that ceremony."

Missus Cruncietti looked at them with wistful eyes. "At times that man I married is still there. I can still see him. I guess I just want my Mitch back so much…"

126

Mario went over and put a compassionate arm around his mother. "That's what we all want, Mom. To have Dad back, just the way he was."

"If we kept him home," their mother asked, "they would send us the plaque they would have given him at the ceremony, wouldn't they?"

"Of course, Mom," replied Mario.

She smiled. "I'm glad. That's something he might be able to understand."

Just then they heard the sound of footsteps. Mitch bounded in to join them. "Hey gang," he said, "how come you're pickin' through my mail?"

CHAPTER 19

Rudy checked out the Inland Valley College Website and observed that they were going to induct into its hall of fame a couple of alumnae who competed unsuccessfully in the Summer Olympics.

But what about Mitch?

Naturally, Mitch's reply to the letter would have arrived late, so maybe that explained everything. Rudy gave himself a little pat on the back for having driven out to Yardbird and seen Hoss, who told him about the induction ceremony; otherwise the Cruncietti family would have remained ignorant of the College's desire to honor Mitch.

Rudy sat back in the Claymore High library and vegged out for a few minutes. He looked out the window and saw a few scudding clouds and noticed that a slight breeze ruffled the trees. A few students passed by the window, smiled and waved. He waved back. They knew him from his heroics on the football field, the guy who ripped big holes for Joe Rossi to run through. He guessed that most of his classmates had forgiven him for being the cocky kid with the funny accent who came to school thumping his chest like Tarzan and saying, in effect, "I am your new quarterback. Worship me."

But Mario remained their quarterback and Rudy accepted the humbling job of blocker for Rossi, and the Pioneers got some help it didn't need but quite appreciated anyway.

One of the girls who passed by the library's window was Lauren. In her tight Levi's and T-shirt, she looked cuter and sweeter than ever. *How wonderful life is now you're in the world.* Then she walked away and Kimberley appeared. The Cruncietti girl made eye contact with him, offered him the subtlest of nods and strode on.

Well, he thought, I probably won't be getting a Christmas card from the Crunciettis. I thought I was looking out for Mitch and that his family was cool with that, but not right now. Also, Rudy sensed that something was up, so he went back to the College Website and looked around some more. No mention of Mitch anywhere. That meant the big man wasn't going to be at that ceremony.

Rudy hustled out of the library and caught up with Kimberley as she stood in line in the cafeteria.

"You're keeping him home," he muttered into the girl's ear over the din of kids' chatter.

She nodded.

"How come?"

"It's none of your business," she said.

"Pretend it *is* my business. Talk to me anyway."

Kimberley looked this way and that, and Rudy could practically see her brain whirring as she sought out the best thing to say and how to say it. But then she just said, "Sorry, Rudy."

"Save the apology for your dad."

She snarled at him. "Why take him to something

130

he wouldn't understand? Everyone would see that there was something wrong with him. He might get all confused and make a scene."

"Maybe he won't make a scene. Maybe he'll be happy to get all that love."

Kimberley shook her head. "Anyway, it's not up to me. It's my mom's call."

Rudy arched an eyebrow. "Maybe it's Mario's call."

She snarled again. "Back off, Maxa. I know you and my brother have this thing going, this rivalry, and I have issues with him, too. But he is my family and you are not, and we know our father better than you ever will, so stop acting like you're the third Cruncietti sibling."

Rudy nodded and shrugged, helpless before the truth.

"You're right," he muttered. "It's none of my business. See ya." He left the cafeteria.

Rudy admitted to himself that he had no right to stick his nose into the Crunciettis' crisis, yet he believed that he, as Mitch's friend—to the extent that either guy had any "friends"—had insights into the man's character that his spouse and offspring lacked. Rudy's relationship with Mitch, in many ways, was a sorry, sad joke—but wasn't it a friendship, anyway? Rudy felt sure that it was, especially when he reminded himself that he was up on charges for refusing to snitch Mitch off.

Over the past while, Rudy had thought a great deal about Mitch-and-Hoss and how Mitch had replaced that with Mitch-and-Rudy. Mitch and Hoss had grown up together, had played football, chased girls and slept in the park when they got hammered and their folks wouldn't let them come home. Now Mitch was about to miss out on the biggest honor to come to him in a very long time.

Well, what would Hoss have done?

Kimberley insisted that her dad was so addled by Alzheimer's that he would fail to understand what was happening at the ceremony and might actually lose control of himself. Rudy could see how opinionated the girl was; he could talk to her till his face turned blue and she wouldn't budge on keeping Mitch home on induction night. Could be she was right about her father, but there was always the chance she was wrong.

He thought, *Why don't I go ask the person who knows for sure?*

Rudy felt weirded out as he pulled into Burned Out Park in the middle of the day. He felt totally OK about ditching school but suspected that if Officer Michaelson discovered him here, the cop would bust him for truancy in addition to vandalism and harassment. This thing—being in trouble with the fuzz—was new to Rudy, and he didn't like it at all. *He* was no criminal, and he resented being treated like one.

He saw more people than usual—moms pushing strollers, old folks yakking away at each other; at times he'd wondered if he and Mitch were the only ones who knew of its existence. He looked at a couple of aged men arguing on a bench near the Bronze Horse. Rudy pictured Mitch reclining on that big beast, waiting for his buddy to show up so that they could kick each other's butt. Back then, Mitch was about the only person in Claymore, California who

132

would spend any time with the new kid in town.

Not that Rudy's social life had improved much since then.

Mitch, come play with me. Nobody here likes me.

He knew that he would have to go back to Claymore High before the school day was over. But before he did so, he got back into his car and cruised through Mitch's neighborhood.

He had just left the park and had his windows rolled down when he heard a racket somewhere on the street. He glanced around and figured out that the trouble was coming from a city bus. The big vehicle had stopped, its doors sat open and about a dozen people stood waiting to board.

A big man stepped off the bus and whirled around. "I paid my money! I'm supposed to get a ride!"

"You paid a quarter!" came a voice from inside the bus. "The fare is two dollars!"

"Two dollars? Just for a bus ride? That's outrageous!"

"It is what it is, pal. You don't hear anyone else complainin'."

Rudy swung his Passat into the nearest space and hopped out. He ran up to the big guy and said, "What's the deal?"

Mitch glowered at him. "Don't try to jump the line, kid."

The red-faced bus driver said, "Do you know this guy? Is he anyone to you?"

"Uncle," Rudy replied.

"Get him a doctor or something, OK? He's done this before. Sometimes he ends up at the mall with no idea of how he got there or how to get home."

Rudy nodded. "Come on, Mitch. Let's go to Burned Out Park or something."

"Who are you?" Mitch asked, sneering. "Don't be orderin' me around."

Rudy smiled. "It's just me, Mitch. I'm Hoss."

Mitch scratched his head.

"Mitch, let's go see that doofus and bug him for a while."

Rudy took a couple of steps towards Burned Out Park and Mitch followed. Soon the two began sauntering down the street, Mitch looking right and left, grinning as he took in the familiar scenery.

"Maybe we shouldn't hassle Doofus," Mitch said. "Let's find someone else to bug."

"Look, Mitch, I need to talk to you about something."

Mitch dribbled an imaginary ball and shot it into an invisible basket. "Talk, Hoss."

"Do the letters I.V.C. mean anything to you?"

Mitch shrugged. "Inland Valley College. Went to school there."

"Have fun?"

"Too much. You were there."

"Sure. We're the same age."

"Couple of weeks apart."

So far, so good, Rudy thought. Go for it. "Mitch, how would you feel if the College inducted you into its sports hall of fame? Would you attend the ceremony?"

Mitch beamed at him. "Me? In their hall of fame? Sign me up!"

Rudy thought, and thought, and thought some more,

but his conclusions were always thus:

Mitch needed to go to Inland Valley College for its induction ceremony.

His family refused to take him there.

Rudy would have to drive Mitch to the ceremony.

Doing so would be quite a big deal. The Pioneers' biggest game of the year, against the Gus Robertson Titans, happened on the same day as the ceremony. Also, he couldn't tell his team that he had other plans not including them, because such a revelation would invite a dozen questions he didn't want to answer.

He had done his best to show the Pioneers that he was the quarterback they needed, and when Coach Hartman made him a blocker instead, he accepted that position with as much aplomb as he could. By failing to play in that crucial game against the Titans, he would be risking all that he had worked for.

As difficult as that would probably be, it was a minor issue compared to the challenges of spending a day with an Alzheimer's victim. That was the sort of adventure that would certainly attract plenty of attention. The College had scheduled its hall-of-fame induction ceremony for halftime at its homecoming football game; even if Mitch and Rudy took off at the conclusion of the ceremony, they would be gone quite a little while, and Mitch's family always got anxious whenever he went away for more than an hour without saying where he had gone or with whom.

Plus, when Mitch's family figured out that he had gone with Rudy to Inland Valley College *without their knowledge and against their wishes*, Rudy thought it would be real interesting to see how they would react.

Rudy shook his head, shrugged and blew out a

huge breath. His plan, whatever faults it had, was also *the right thing to do*. He was playing the part of Hoss, Mitch's best friend, and as such needed to deliver the Inland Valley College alumnus to receive this athletics honor.

The *delivery* of Mitch to the College would be simple enough; he'd just stow the guy into the passenger's seat, roll up the windows and jack up the air conditioning—Mitch loved the cold air as much as Rudy did—and zoom off to the campus, over 100 miles away. But then he remembered the knocking and pinging from underneath the VW's hood, and decided that having a mechanical breakdown on the freeway with Mitch would be quite nightmarish. *So*, he thought, *what are my other options?*

He called Michael Hossman.

"Hoss, I need a favor."

"Name it."

"Are you still going to that hall of fame ceremony?"

Hoss laughed. "Sure am. After our visit, I keep thinking about Mitch and all those good times from years back."

"Well, would you mind driving Mitch and me to that ceremony?"

"Thought you already had a ride. How did you get all the way out here to Yardbird?"

"Yeah, I do have a car, but it's been acting up lately and I can't afford a mechanic right now. I just don't want my car to crap out on the highway in the middle of nowhere with Mitch in the passenger's seat. He might not understand."

"I hear that. Sure, Rudy, I can give you fellas a lift. But why isn't Mitch going to the ceremony with his family? Don't they want to be there with him?"

"The deal is, Claymore High has a big game against the Titans on that day, and Mitch's son Mario is the Pioneers' quarterback. So, because none of them can be in two places at once, they decided that Mitch would go get his induction while his family went to the football game."

"Well, that makes sense, I guess. Doesn't surprise me that Mitch's son is a Pioneer. I could never get my boys that interested in football, even though they're big and strong like their old man." Then, "I'm sure looking forward to seeing Mitch again, even if he says, 'Who's this guy? Never seen him in my life.' Where should I pick you up?"

Rudy gave his own address. He didn't like the idea of having Hoss pull up at Mitch's house, nor did he consider Burned Out Park an ideal pickup location.

All that remained for Rudy was to wait and hope that Mitch was still mentally together enough to be at the right place at the right time.

CHAPTER 21

The Crunciettis' front door swung open and Mario stepped out, pulling on his Pioneers letterman jacket. "Chop, chop, Kimberley!" he yelled in the direction of his kid sister's bedroom as he headed to his car.

"Need a few minutes," she yelled back.

"Gonna leave without you!" he shouted as he fired up his Camaro.

"Right behind you!" She emerged from the house as she dug through her knapsack. This dispute, such as it was, occurred each morning, and this one was not so bad; often Mario ended up inching down the street, honking his horn and threatening to zoom off alone as Kimberley waved for him to stop as she pulled her comb through her hair or adjusted the strap of her brassiere. At no time did either sibling seem to consider cutting the other some slack.

Rudy, crouching behind the abundant shrubbery of a house close to the Crunciettis', watched the girl half-fall into the moving car and nearly lose a shoe as she shut its door. He also heard her scream something at her brother but couldn't make out what. This was the third or fourth consecutive morning Rudy had hidden behind the bushes and watched the

Cruncietti kids leave for school. His goal was to ensure that on the big day he would know Mitch's routine well enough to gather him up and take him away to get his hall of fame induction. Rudy knew that Alzheimer's victims were predictably unpredictable. Even four-legged brutes in the wilderness, who wore no wristwatches and had no wall clocks to look at, did the same things and went to the same places at the same times.

Rudy smiled as he spotted Mitch step out and settle himself on the porch swing. The old guy unfolded the morning paper, spent maybe two seconds looking at it, then put it aside. He began peeling an orange, ate some and set it, too, aside.

He frowned at the sight of Mitch's down-filled Raiders jacket in this mild weather. What was up with *that*? But then Missus Cruncietti appeared with a windbreaker draped over her arm. She got her hubby to stand up, removed his heavy jacket and replaced it with the lighter one. Then she bussed him on the forehead and went back inside. Mitch stood up and began jogging.

Rudy sneaked back into his VW and followed Mitch, staying a block behind. He knew that Mitch as likely as not would fail to recognize the car or its driver even if Rudy cruised right alongside him. Mitch always headed for Burned Out Park—in what passed for downtown Claymore—and as he got closer to the park and people, he reminded Rudy of a young, spunky dog eager to take it all in, to urinate on every bush and enjoy a tummy scratch from everyone inclined to provide one.

As he checked the time, Rudy reminded himself that Claymore High was still in session and his presence there was still required. He had already missed two consecutive Spanish classes, and a third ditch would result in a phone call to Missus Maxa: "Hey! Where's your boy?" She would go ballistic. He had already caused her much grief by getting into trouble with the cops, and he supposed that there would be consequences for taking Mitch to that hall of fame ceremony. My mom is much too good to me, Rudy thought.

He decided on a course of action: Go to Spanish class, then get back into his car and return to downtown to see how long it would take to find Mitch again as the old guy wandered this way and that throughout Claymore.

But Rudy felt full of anxiety as Spanish class ended and he hurried back to his VW. He drove downtown; no Mitch. He headed over to Burned Out Park; no Mitch. Then he tooled around town—up and down the streets he had never troubled himself to visit before—when he heard shouting and pounding. He looked around and saw a big man pounding on an Inland Valley Bank ATM.

Rudy pulled over to the side. "What's the deal?"

Mitch spun around, his face livid with rage. "I put my money in and didn't get my candy bar! I'm hungry!" He kicked the machine and it made a sort of whimpering noise, the kind of sound a boy might make after being kicked in the scrotum.

Rudy got out of his car. "The problem," he said, "is that this is a money machine, not a candy machine."

"Well, I put my money in and got nothing. No candy bar, no money back, no nothing."

Rudy looked at the machine and saw a Susan B.

141

Anthony dollar coin jammed in a slot. "Not a candy machine, Mitch. You want a candy bar? I'll buy you one." He put a gentle hand on Mitch's arm and led him towards the VW.

Mitch eyeballed him. "You know my name? We know each other from somewhere?"

"I'm Rudy Maxa. I moved here from Indiana."

"Indiana? I've been there. I went there when I played football." Then, "You own this car?"

"I own it and the bank owns me."

Mitch laughed. "Well, I've been thinking of getting a car myself. I think I have one already, but I don't know where it is. Maybe I'll just buy a new one."

Rudy opened the passenger's-side door. "Get in."

Mitch did as told and as soon as they were both seated and belted in, he blasted the air conditioner.

"Nice and cold!" Mitch shouted.

Rudy smiled. He felt pretty happy himself; he always did when driving around with the windows up and the frigid air in his face. As they drove along the fence enclosing Burned Out Park, Mitch checked out the trees he knew so well. Then he turned to Rudy.

"Hoss, why didn't you tell me you had a car?"

CHAPTER 22

The weather on the big day was partly cloudy, with a brisk breeze—and Rudy loved it. Great weather for Claymore High's against the Gus Robertson Titans and Inland Valley College's homecoming.

Rudy sat in his car at the end of Mitch's street, checking the time over and over. Where *was* the old dude? After so many covert visits to this neighborhood, Rudy figured he knew Mitch's comings and goings very well, and the guy should have come outside by now.

In less than half an hour, Michael Hossman would pull up in his Caddy to collect Rudy and Mitch at Rudy's house for the drive out to the college...and nobody would be at home.

What was up with that? Had Mitch's family decided not to let him walk or jog alone any longer? Rudy thought they would probably be wise to do such a thing, but why would they start doing so today? As long as Rudy had known him, Mitch had gone out by himself and, somehow, had always managed to find his way back home. So far as the Crunciettis were concerned, today should be just like all the others.

But apparently it wasn't.

Rudy felt like a spy, or a criminal, as he tiptoed to the Crunciettis' basement window, quite unsure of what he might find. What he found, which at once pleased and disheartened him, was the sight of Mitch sitting in a recliner, nodding and smiling as music played. Rudy closed his eyes and pressed his ear to the glass. The Rolling Stones, it sounded like. Well, he thought, the old boy has totally forgotten me. Surprise, surprise. Gotta act fast.

He tapped on the window. Mitch looked up, got up and went over to see who was there.

"Who you? What you want?"

"It's Hoss, Mitch. Let's go. They're waiting for us."

"What for?"

"Your friends and admirers. They wanna say hi."

Mitch shrugged. "OK, let's do it."

He hauled himself through the basement window with little effort. Rudy was about to suggest using the front door like everyone else, but he didn't want to confuse his friend any further.

The two scampered over to Rudy's Passat. Mitch said, "Have we met? I'm Mitch Cruncietti." He extended his hand.

"I'm Rudy Maxa." He shook Mitch's hand.

Mitch shook his head. "Don't know any Rudy Maxa."

"Then I'm Mike Hossman."

Mitch brightened. "Oh, sure! Hoss! How come you're out this way?"

"I've come to take you to see some old friends.

They want to say hi."

"Old friends are the best friends," Mitch said as he got into the car. "Is this thing a piece of junk, or can it really move?"

"It goes as fast as it needs to go." He drove fast, wanting to get home as soon as possible. Hoss would probably be there already, thinking that Rudy's house was the Cruncietti residence. The best thing, Rudy decided, was for them to get to his house right away, pile into Hoss's Caddy and take off for the ceremony without much conversation along the way.

When they reached Rudy's house, he pulled his VW into the garage, noticing with relief that the Caddy hadn't arrived. The two guys waited a few minutes in the driveway until the big gleaming Seville rolled up. Michael Hossman got out and cried out, "Mitch! It's been years!"

"Hey, wassup," Mitch replied, climbing into the Caddy as if he were a child checking out a new toy.

"Is he having a good day or a bad one?" Hoss asked Rudy.

"More good than bad. Just keep saying stuff like, 'We're going to see some old friends and say hi.'"

"Then we better hurry up. Seems to me we've got the man of the evening here, so we better be on time."

Rudy got into the back seat and Hoss arranged his big, long body in the driver's seat. Presently they were on the streets that led to the highway; Rudy worried for a moment about the long drive and what sort of conversation might happen. But then Hoss slipped a CD of Inland Valley College's fight songs into the Caddy's player and the two men began to sing along.

Behind them, Rudy sat back and laughed as Mitch leaned forward to turn up the air conditioner. Hoss didn't object. The kid from Indiana could scarcely believe that Mitch, whose memory seemed so full of holes, could remember these college songs he hadn't heard in decades.

The music ended and the two men guffawed as if at the punch line of a dirty joke. "I found a cassette of those songs and made a CD of them just for fun," Hoss said, his belly still shaking. "The older we get, the better we were. Right, pal?"

"Right. Remember when the guy at the liquor store sold us Schlitz Malt Liquor even though we were underage? We got drunk and our folks wouldn't let us come home so we had to sleep in that friggin' park."

Hoss nodded. "Happened more than once, as I recall."

"Didn't get a good night's sleep on those benches, either."

"But we survived." Hoss tapped Mitch on the arm. "Anyway, we got to talk about the greatest stunt ever pulled. That stunt was courtesy of one Mitch Cruncietti."

Rudy sat up and leaned forward. "Do tell!"

"Which stunt you talkin' about?" Mitch asked.

"The Renfrew game. They had that falcon. They called it Fanny."

"I gotta hear this," said Rudy.

"Well," said Hoss, "we played for Inland Valley College and our archrivals were from Renfrew College. Their team was the Raptors and their mascot was Fanny, this big, ugly falcon that wouldn't shut up. We hated that bird almost as much as we hated that

146

team and its school. But Mitch was the guy who said, 'Let's do something about ol' Fanny.'"

Mitch shrugged. "I stole the cage."

"Don't be so modest. While this big argument happens on the field about a blown call or something, Mitch, while no one's paying him any attention, swipes the cage with Fanny in it and starts sprinting up the stairs of the stands. The Raptors see him and start running after him! They're gonna kill him! The falcon is going crazy, too!"

"I just had a job to do," Mitch said.

"He gets to the back row and hops onto the cement wall. No one can touch him—if he falls, it's 'Goodbye, Mitch.' So what does he do? He starts singing, 'Fly Like an Eagle,' and he opens the cage and Fanny flies off!"

Mitch nodded. "I did the right thing. It was inhumane to keep that bird caged up like that."

"Did you get in trouble?" Rudy asked.

"Yes and no. Everyone was, like, 'Shame on you! Shame on you!' but they didn't actually *do* anything to me. You can get away with all kinds of stuff when you're a college football star."

"Did you guys at least beat the Raptors?" Rudy asked.

Hoss laughed. "No way. They creamed us. We knew they would, too. But from that day forward, whenever I went to that stadium, I would look up to see if Fanny had come back. Didn't you, Mitch?"

"Not me," Mitch said with a chuckle. "I would have been mad at that bird for coming back after I'd done it the biggest favor of its life. All living things should be free."

"I'm thirsty," said Rudy. "You fellas think we have

147

time to stop somewhere for a soda or something?"

Rudy was glad that they took a break for refreshments. They pulled into one of the dozen or so truck stops along the highway and sat down for pie and coffee. Mitch shoveled away his apple pie like a man who truly appreciated goodies. He also seemed mentally together as he and Hoss yakked about the good, bad and ugly restaurants they'd visited as college boys on the road. "This one place in Oregon?" Mitch said. "The meals we had made us sick. Our center had the farts so bad that the quarterback hated taking the snaps from him."

Hoss and Rudy howled. Sitting there together, years after that game—Hoss a prosperous lawyer and Mitch an Alzheimer's victim—the two men, despite no contact for the longest time, could still enjoy each other's company.

Looking at his watch, Hoss said, "Well, this has been fun, but we have to boogie. They're expecting us down yonder so they can give Mitch a standing ovation."

"Before we do that," Mitch said, "I better give them back some of this coffee. Where's the restroom?"

Rudy and Hoss waited in the parking lot while Mitch relieved himself.

"You weren't exaggerating about his deterioration," Hoss told Rudy. "One moment he seems really together, but the next moment he's totally confused."

"Yeah. Thanks for doing this. It means a lot to me."

"Thanks ain't necessary. He and I were so tight for so many years, I just assumed we would be friends for life. When we went our separate ways, I didn't bother to contact him at all. I really haven't been much of a friend to him, mainly because I was too busy with other things. It's sad to see what's happened to him."

"He's been in the can for a little while now," Rudy said. "Hope he's not constipated."

"Or worse. Let's go see."

They entered the men's room and found no Mitch. He had taken off.

CHAPTER 23

Hoss shook his head in disbelief. "We shouldn't have let him go to the men's room by himself. Why would he abandon us like that?"

"Because," Rudy replied, "he probably had already forgotten we were here with him."

The two guys stared at each other for a moment. Hoss said, "would he head for the hills?"

Rudy replied, "I don't think he's running away. I think he got confused, forgot he was with us, and now he needs to get back home."

Hoss nodded and they walked a little ways along the highway.

"There he is." Rudy pointed to a lone figure hitching a ride.

"Better get him before someone else does."

They hurried towards him, waving and shouting, and watched as a trucker seemed to slow down for the hitcher. But then the driver probably got a good look at his would-be passenger, a tall, powerfully built man, and decided that picking him up might not be the wisest course of action. The big rig picked up speed and roared past the hitchhiker.

Rudy and Hoss ran back to the Caddy, got in and

raced out onto the highway. When they reached Mitch, Hoss stopped.

"Where ya headin', partner?"

Mitch scratched his bald head. "I'm going home. I am an American. I live in California, in the United States."

"Sounds good. Get in."

Mitch nodded and did so. Hoss swallowed hard and shot a weird look at Rudy as if saying, *He wants to go home to America? He lives in California? Where does he think this is, Planet Fringus?*

Rudy shifted and replied with the tiniest shrug.

Hoss said, "I went to Inland Valley College, a zillion years ago."

"So did I! How about that, huh?" Mitch beamed and Hoss rolled his eyes.

"Check this out." Hoss slid the school's fight song CD back into the player, and Mitch started singing again.

"Homecoming tonight," Hoss said.

"That so? Wish I could go."

"Your wish is my command." Hoss drove a little faster and turned up the air conditioning. Mitch smiled.

Mario stuffed his things into his duffel bag and asked, "Where's Dad?"

"Gone out for his run," Kimberley said.

"He'll be back soon," said their mother. "He knows it's a big game for Mario."

"This is *Dad* we're talking about. He, uh, forgets. Like, all the time. I can't imagine where he is right now."

152

"That's disrespectful," said Kimberley.

"Just tellin' it like it is."

"Go meet up with your jock pals," Kimberley said. "I'm sure Dad will turn up in time to see you play football."

"I'm not sure of that at all," Mario said.

CHAPTER 24

As they arrived at Inland Valley College, Mitch looked every which way, Rudy thought, *He knows this place. I'm not sure if he understands that he's being honored tonight, but he knows this campus and maybe he'll know some of these people. Maybe he won't freak them out and they won't freak him out.*

"Good ol' I.V.C.," Hoss said. "Somehow it looks different—less imposing—than it did way back when. Huh, Mitch?"

He pointed to his right. "Used to be a statue there. Wonder what they did with it."

"While we're wondering about that," said Hoss, "let's wonder about getting to the stadium. That's sort of our destination."

Minutes later, they were inching along in a lineup. Then Rudy pointed to a sign saying V.I.P. ENTRANCE.

"That's for us," he said.

"Yeah." Hoss smiled. "We've got Captain Crunch in here with us."

At the gate, the attendant said, "You're not on our list."

"Don't know anything about a list," Hoss

retorted. "But I got a V.I.P. sitting right next to me."

The attendant squinted at Mitch for a moment; then an older woman wearing a blue suit and plastic badge came over and said, "Mitch Cruncietti! I was afraid you weren't going to come!" To the attendant she said, "Why didn't you wave them right on through? Can't you see it's Mitch Cruncietti in there?"

"Is that so? I didn't recognize him. May I shake your hand, Mitch?"

As the attendant beamed and pumped Mitch's hand, Rudy gave himself a small pat on the back for making this thing happen. *This is the greatest moment of my life.*

Rudy was so wrapped up in feeling great about this evening that it took him a moment to realize that the attendant and lady were taking Mitch away.

"Hold up!" Hoss hollered, standing between Mitch and those who wished to take him away. "Where we go, he goes—and vice versa."

The woman shook her head. "Negative. There's no room for you and that young fellow."

"'Negative'? I repeat: He and we are inseparable this evening, period."

The woman laughed. "Are you Siamese twins or something?"

"We are his entourage."

They reached a compromise: Rudy and Hoss would sit a couple of rows behind Mitch so that they could hustle him away if he freaked out. Mitch sat between a brother-and-sister team who had graduated from the school and skated in the Olympics. Next to them sat the president of Inland Valley College.

As those in attendance learned that the retired Raider had shown up, they formed a line to say hello.

Each well-wisher received a firm handshake, a big smile and a sincere "Good to see ya!" Rudy felt sure that nobody there could tell there was anything wrong with him—Mitch Cruncietti, so far as anyone could tell, was exactly as he appeared to be—a big, proud alumnus, a retired NFL player who was content in middle age to come out tonight and say hi to the folks.

Hoss muttered to Rudy, "Check him out. An hour or so ago he thought he was on Planet Fringus. Now he's acting like he's running for office. Go figure."

"Let's hope he can keep his head together for the rest of the evening."

"Amen to that."

Kimberley came home and called out, "Is Dad back yet?"

Her mother came in from the kitchen. "I take it you didn't find him."

"No, and I looked, like, *everywhere*. I even went to Burned Out Park, where pervy old coots sit around all day. They were checking me out. Yuck!"

"Well, Mario's game isn't for a few hours. There's still time."

Kimberley shook her head. "You don't get it! Dad is on his own schedule. He does his own thing. He's been taken out of his environment, and who knows what kind of trouble he could get into?"

Virginia Cruncietti nodded. "I hear that. But the thing is, he's gone off before but he's always come back. This isn't that big a deal."

"Oh? Remember the time we had, like, *no* idea

where he had gone, and Rudy had to go get him and bring him home." Then, "It got to where we had to hide his car keys because we couldn't trust him behind the wheel. Now it's like we're getting to where we can't let him go outside by himself. Or maybe we're already at that point, but it's too late. He could be dead as we speak."

Missus Cruncietti put her hands on her hips. "Don't overreact, Kimberley. Don't be jumping to conclusions like that."

"Shouldn't we call Mario about now and tell him we haven't located Dad yet?"

"Nope. Dad's just a little late—he may turn up any minute. Calling Mario and getting him all upset unnecessarily would accomplish nothing, especially since today is the biggest game of the year for him."

"Well, what*ever!*" Kimberley, her face crimson, swung around and marched to her bedroom. After mutely calling her mother a half-dozen vile names, she admitted to herself that her mom was simply trying to be optimistic...but *optimism* was far different from *realism*. How could she be, like, "Don't worry. He'll show up. If something tragic has happened to him, we'll start worrying then"? Kimberley thought back to the night of that party at Grant Miller's house; if Rudy hadn't been there and taken charge of the situation, her father probably would have been killed.

Rudy. He was the only one left who seemed to have much use for Kimberley's dad. Rudy knew how to handle the old guy, or at least could advise the Crunciettis on what to do whenever Mitch ran away. She felt pretty sure that her father wasn't at Burned Out Park, but Rudy might know where he might be, and she knew she would feel better about things if she called him.

She tried his cell and got no answer. She called his mother at work.

"Missus Maxa, my name is Kimberley Cruncietti—"

"You're Mitch's daughter."

"Yes, ma'am."

"Mario's sister."

"Yes, ma'am. I'm trying to locate Rudy. Any idea where he is?"

"Have you tried his cell?"

Duh. "He's not answering it."

"Then I don't know what o say. He told me he would be gone all day to see a football game…"

Kimberley frowned. Rudy was going to *see* a football game? Wasn't he supposed to *play* football today alongside Mario? And didn't Mario depend heavily upon Rudy to block for Joe Rossi?

Then she figured it out. There was a *college* football game that day. Kimberley turned on her computer and went to Inland Valley College's Website. They had a live stream of their homecoming game versus Renfrew College. The camera panned the crowd, and Kimberley let out a cry.

"What is it?" called her mother.

"Dad's at the game."

"The game hasn't started yet."

"Not that game. The one we wouldn't let him go to."

Missus Cruncietti entered the room and Kimberley pointed at her monitor.

"Inland Valley College? How did he get there?"

"I guess," Kimberley replied, "that you-know-who took him."

159

"I *don't* know who." Missus Cruncietti sighed. "I'm totally confused."

They watched some more, and presently saw, sitting not far from Mitch, Rudy Maxa.

Officer Bruce Michaelson rested the telephone in its cradle and thought, *I would write a book about what I see and hear as a cop, but nobody would believe it.*

This time, the call was about a high schooler who had taken a fiftysomething Alzheimer's victim to attend a football game where they were going to honor the Alzheimer's person. Problem was, the man's family had forbidden him to go and they wanted the teenager arrested for kidnapping, or abduction, or *something.* Michaelson was unclear as to why the family had refused to let the man attend the game at which he was to be honored…but the cop supposed that that was *not* any of Officer Bruce Michaelson's business.

What else was there? Oh, right—the bad guy was Rudy Maxa, the kid from Indiana who'd just moved out here with his divorced mom. Kathleen Maxa— cute with a capital C. But her kid? He already had a court date for harassment and vandalism beefs.

Michaelson could empathize with the Crunciettis' outrage at Rudy Maxa but, from a legal standpoint the officer wasn't altogether sure that Maxa had done anything wrong. After all, the kid hadn't asked for ransom, and surely would not, so a kidnapping charge probably would not happen. Michaelson suspected that Maxa would take Mitch Cruncietti home after the Inland Valley College game, and the Crunciettis would stay angry for a few days over having their wishes disrespected, then forget the whole matter.

Michaelson had to stop and think for a moment about where Inland Valley College was. Oh yeah—Betts County. He called the Betts County Sheriff's Office and felt relieved when Sergeant Gary Crocker, an old friend, answered the phone.

"Crock, it's Mike. I need a favor."

"Talk to me."

"You have the homecoming game out at the campus right now."

"Sure do. Half the county is there. Wish *I* was there, too."

"Well, one of our more distinguished Claymore folks is there, too."

"Cruncietti."

"Oh, so you know about this?"

"Yep. They tell me they invited him, but he didn't reply, but he showed up anyway. Everyone's pretty tickled to see him." Then, "By the way, why did he show after indicating he wouldn't?"

"That's why I'm calling, Crock. Cruncietti took way too many blows to the head when he played football. He has a pretty advanced case of Alzheimer's, so his family tries to keep him out of situations where people might see how sick he is."

"Want to tell me the name of the kid who took him out to the game today?"

"Negative. I'm not concerned about him. He's in the stands, a couple of rows behind Cruncietti. Mitch is the guy I'm worried about."

"Want me to have campus security escort Cruncietti from the facility?"

"Negative. Let him have his fun. Just make sure he doesn't leave the stadium by himself. I'll be there as soon as I can."

"Roger that." Click.

Michaelson stared at his car keys for a moment or two. He'd really wanted to catch the Pioneers game that day, to see if they could remain undefeated for another week. Instead, he was driving all the way out to Inland Valley College to babysit Cruncietti and Maxa.

The cop hoped, at the very least, that Kathleen Maxa liked him half as much as he liked her.

CHAPTER 25

The brother-sister team who had failed to win medals at the Olympics had succeeded in gaining some weight, but they stood and waved, all smiles and pride. On the stadium screens, footage of the siblings at the Games drew applause and cheers.

Then came Mitch's turn. Images of him in his I.V.C. football uniform, then Mitch as a Raider. The big man sat on the stage and watched along with everyone else as Rudy, from his grandstand seat, watched Mitch, wondering how much, if any, of this tribute the ex-footballer comprehended.

"Ladies and gentlemen, please welcome our other Hall of Fame inductee, Inland Valley College alumnus and former Oakland Raiders linebacker, Mitch 'Captain Crunch' Cruncietti!"

The stadium's air fairly vibrated with love for Mitch. Everyone gave a standing ovation to the Claymore son who had gone from Inland Valley College to snap up two Super Bowl rings while playing for the silver and black.

The school's president gestured for Mitch to step up to the microphone, and after a moment's hesitation, the big man did exactly that. Rudy felt his heart pound and pulse race; he looked over at Hoss, who gave him the tiniest shrug. Both guys leaned forward, shoulders hunch tight, ready for whatever blather came from Mitch's maw.

"It's so good to be back at Inland Valley, the finest college nobody's ever heard of!"

The crowd roared and stamped its feet. It carried on like so for the next ten minutes.

"The last time I was on this field, Shelley Ruddick had given me the gift that keeps on giving, and in return I had stolen her undies and run them up the flagpole." The crowd laughed some more. "That's just my way of saying that my time here was something I will forever remember as one of the happiest of my life. For you to have me back here today to honor me? Well, that's just a huge bonus. Thank you so much!"

Hoss leaned over. "Rudy, he gets it! He knows what's goin' on!"

Rudy smiled. "Yeah, and shame on his family for wanting to keep him home!"

The cheers and applause seemed to go on forever.

Back in Claymore, Virginia Cruncietti wiped tears from her eyes. "That was the man I married. Before he got sick."

Kimberley nodded. "It's like he came back from the dead."

Her mother snuffled. "I often don't realize how much of him we've lost until I see him when he's fairly lucid."

"He looks so *blissful* out there. He's just totally

together." Kimberley snarled. "That dork Rudy! Why is it that he's always right when it comes to Dad?"

"I'm the one who refused to do the right thing for your father," said Missus Cruncietti.

"Doesn't matter now. Dad's all smiles. Everyone out there loves him."

Rudy and Hoss wiped away their own tears as they stood with the others, alternately applauding Mitch and high-fiving each other.

Rudy felt he had much to feel proud of. He had gone to so much trouble—and angered many people—just to get Mitch here for this special moment, and it happened. It really happened! His life so recently had been full of bad experiences and unhappy emotions: Resentment of his father, ambivalence about his decision not to pursue a relationship with Lauren...and of course his poor relationships with Mario, Kimberley and Coach Hartman. He even got mad at his mother for taking him out of Indiana. But this time he did something and knew it was absolutely, positively *right*.

He watched as the grounds crew moved the stage back to where it had come from. The brother and sister inducted into the hall of fame had gone off. So, apparently, had Mitch.

"Where *is* he?" Rudy asked, grabbing Hoss by the shoulder.

"He can't have gone far. Remember what he was wearing?"

"A college jacket, like most of the old guys here right now."

They got out of their seats and headed down to

the field.

A security guard spotted them. "You're unauthorized personnel! Return to your seats!"

"We need to find Mitch Cruncietti!" hollered Hoss.

"Back to your seats!"

Just then Rudy spotted Mitch on the other side of the gridiron, entering the tunnel from which the Renfrew College players were emerging. Mitch darted past them; Rudy waited until the players had left the tunnel, then hurried inside. No Mitch. Hoss caught up with them, and the two called, "Mitch! Mitch!" as they wandered through the innards of the stadium.

"The locker rooms...the equipment storage...the VIP parking lot," said Rudy as he ran through his hair. "What's your guess?"

"Parking lot."

Outside, they saw a young lady sitting on the grass.

"Excuse me," said Hoss, "but have you seen a big, bald guy about my age? He may seem a bit confused."

"Well," she replied, "there was someone matching that description tramping around in the fountain over there a little while ago. He even stopped to take a leak in the pool. Then he tried to climb the statue, but the pigs came and took him away."

Hoss groaned.

"Well, at least now we know he's in someone's custody," said Rudy. "Where would they have gone?"

"To the security office over there."

They sprinted to their destination. Rudy hoped that he and Hoss could get Mitch out to the stadium and back home to Claymore without any fuss or hassles, but now he figured that the security folks would be full of questions about how Mitch had gotten there and why. As soon as Rudy and Hoss burst into the security office, they saw Mitch sitting on a bench, huddled in a big blanket.

"Rudy Maxa," said a voice.

Rudy turned around to face Officer Bruce Michaelson's ugly face. Then he looked at his pal. "You hangin' in there, Mitch?"

He watched Mitch look at him, then Michaelson, then him again, as if just trying to figure out things. Rudy guessed that Mitch had already forgotten why we was there, who these men were and why they were paying so much attention to him.

"Mitch is hanging in there just fine," Michaelson said. "And he's hanging out with *me*. Maxa, I don't know what to make of you. Maybe you should never have left Indiana in the first place."

Hoss said, "Don't be nasty to Rudy. He just made arrangements for us to drive out here together so that Mitch could get this honor."

Michaelson arched an eyebrow. "And who might *you* be?"

"Michael Hossman, attorney-at-law."

Mitch shook his head. "You can't be!" He pointed at Rudy. "Hoss is a young feller!"

Rudy said, "Mitch, here's how it is: That man is Hoss, your old pal. You two are the same age. You keep calling me Hoss, but I'm Rudy Maxa. I'm seventeen years old."

"Also," Michaelson said, to no one in particular, "Mister Cruncietti isn't supposed to be here. His family decided that he would be better off with them today, but Mister Maxa decided to take him out here instead."

Rudy nodded. "It's all true."

"My experience in dealing with Rudy here," said the cop, "is that he pretty much just does his own thing, regardless of how it affects others. Maybe that's how they do things back in Indiana, but this is California, and out here we believe in having some consideration for others."

"Rudy had the best intentions," said Hoss. "He wanted what was best for Mitch. You shouldn't arrest him for having good intentions."

"Have I arrested anyone?" Michaeslon asked. "Mister Cruncietti is alive and well and will be returning to his family very soon. But what if something tragic had happened to him? Who would have been at fault then? I don't think Mister Maxa thought too much about that when he decided to 'borrow' the man for the day and take him out here."

Rudy closed his eyes and pictured Mitch falling from the statue, hitting his head and losing consciousness and drowning. Or climbing out of the water, clothing soaked, and wandering around Inland Valley College in a hypothermic state as people gawked at the big, strange man, all of them too afraid to offer him help.

"The Crunciettis," said the cop, "have the legal right to press charges. I could bust the two of you right now—"

"I wanna go home!" Mitch cried out in a child's voice. "I'm hungry and tired, and my mom's gonna wonder where I am."

After a prolonged and awkward pause, Officer Michaelson said, "I hear ya, Mitch. Here's what we're gonna do: These nice folks who work here are gonna fetch you some dry clothes to put on, and then I'm gonna drive you back home in my car."

Yeah, Rudy thought, *are you gonna handcuff him too so he can't bust out of your cruiser and run away?*

"We'll be right behind you," Hoss said. "C'mon, Rudy. Our big day is a done deal."

"I hear that."

CHAPTER 26

The stadium at Claymore High School was minuscule, naturally, compared to that of Inland Valley College, but the Pioneers' fans packed in there butt to butt and their excitement became palpable as kickoff time neared.

The Gus Robertson Titans had bused in a few dozen fans to cheer them on. The Titans, despised by the Pioneers and everyone else associated with Claymore High, had been the last team to defeat the Pioneers and seemed the most likely to end that team's unbeaten streak. During his brief time in town, Rudy, as accustomed as he was to the Hoosiers' rivalries, often marveled at how much these two teams—and schools—hated each other.

Kimberley walked around the stands, frowning and shaking her head in the most abject confusion. Even though her classrooms were just a two-minute walk away, she felt as if she were on the other side of the world, surrounded by people whose conversations sounded to her like so much babble. She supposed her sudden alienation from the sports field and football came from her knowledge that football was the source of her father's medical problems.

She noticed her brother at the sidelines, checking out the section of the stands where their parents usually sat. Normally, he was so engrossed in Being the Best Quarterback Who Ever Was that he seemed scarcely aware even of having parents.

She scampered over to him and called out, "Mario!"

He turned to her and mouthed, *Where is Dad?*

"Uh, he's going to be late."

"How late? Why?"

"Let's take this somewhere else."

"Nowhere else to go," he said. "Spill it."

She shrugged. "Don't wig out on me, but he's gone to that I.V.C. deal."

"Oh?" he said, his voice laden with sarcasm. "And how did he get there. Did your *squeeze* drive him?"

Kimberley snarled. "Don't speak to *me* that way. He's not my 'squeeze,' and he's dead freakin' meat when he shows up for school."

"Yeah, I bet. Maxa doesn't give a crap about the Pioneers, so he's a no-show for this game. Instead, he takes *our* dad out to that game *against our wishes*."

Kimberley shook her head. "Negative. I believe he touched base with one of Dad's college friends and the three of them went out there together. The main thing is, Dad's fine. The cops are driving him home."

Mario rolled his eyes. "The cops are driving him home? How did *that* happen?"

"Because we called them. While Mom and I were, like, 'Where's Dad?' I checked on the computer and caught the stream of the Inland Valley game and there he was! He was a missing person to us, so we called the cops. We were afraid that something awful would happen to him. He's so big yet he's so vulnerable."

Mario shook his head. "I don't what Maxa thought he was doing."

"He was doing what he thought was the right thing to do. And I think in many ways he did the right thing by Dad today."

Mario made a face. "Excuse me?"

"Dad went into the Inland Valley College Sports Hall of Fame today and he completely understood it. He even made an acceptance speech and everyone loved it. I downloaded it for you to see."

"Not sure I want to see it," Mario muttered.

"He's probably already forgotten it by now, but so what? When he was younger and more productive, he accomplished plenty, so he deserved and award and some applause. Apparently Rudy Maxa understood that. You, Mom and I did not."

"That guy is bad news," Mario said with a sneer. "He joins our team and he's, like, 'I am your new quarterback. I am the greatest!' Well, no, Maxa, *I'm* the quarterback. So then he starts hitting on Lauren, who sort of happened to be *my* girlfriend, and then he starts making decisions concerning *our* father. Is Dad going to adopt him and leave everything to Maxa? I'm not kidding."

"I can tell." Kimberley's eyes darted here and there. She wondered how many people couldn't help overhearing this "confidential" conversation.

Joe Rossi came up from behind them and said, "Mario—"

The quarterback swung around like a movie tough guy and punched the running back in the facemask. The impact made a horrible noise, and if Rossi hadn't been wearing his helmet, he would have crumpled to the ground, bloodied and unconscious. Instead, he just stood there, staring at Mario.

"What's your *problem*, dude? I just came over to

tell you that Coach says we're ready to go."

Mario, grabbing his right hand, winced in pain. "Can't play today. I broke my hand."

At once, Coach Hartman and Dr. Boyd, who said, "There's some redness but no fracture."

"It's busted. I can tell," said Mario.

"I seriously doubt that," retorted Dr. Boyd.

Coach Hartman took Mario aside and asked, "What's the problem, Cruncietti?"

"My hand's busted. I can't play."

"Boyd says you're good to go."

"He's a freakin' dentist! What does he know?"

Officer Michaelson got a civilian escort back to Claymore, whether he wanted one or not. Hoss and Rudy followed the cop, nearly tailgating him at times.

"I think," Hoss said, "that Mitch has taken a nap. He sort of fell over a few minutes ago, and the day's excitement has probably tuckered him out."

"I'm very sorry about this, Hoss. I got so preoccupied with getting him there for that ceremony that I never stopped to think that I might get you in trouble with the cops."

"Rudy," said Hoss, "if you don't stop saying 'I'm sorry,' I'm gonna punch you in the nose. This honor Mitch got today? It meant even more to me than it did to him."

"But still—we sort of kidnapped the guy and drove him out there. That's illegal—we're lucky that cop didn't bust us."

"I don't regret it for a moment. There are some risks worth taking. I'm a lawyer, so I'm not sure I would have said 'I don't regret breaking the law' yesterday. But I honestly believe that we did the right thing today. Yeah, that hall of fame thing was great, but there was more. We got to see the real Mitch for a little while—we saw the part of him that his disease hadn't touched yet. *You* made that happen for him. You gave him a gift his own family couldn't give him. You would be inducted into the Claymore Humanitarian Hall of Fame if there was such a thing."

Rudy closed his eyes and felt the kiss of very cold air on his face. Yes, Hoss had been kind to say that, and Rudy supposed his words were mostly true. Also, Mitch's day out had been fun and exciting. But he remained a tragic man whose disease kept eating away at his brain. Rudy didn't think there was, or ever would be, a medicine or scientist able to save the Mitch Crunciettis of the world. It was just too sad to think about.

"I think," he said, "I'm gonna keep a low profile for a little while. Our big game against the Titans is, like, right now, and I'm sort of not there. I think Coach Hartman is a little bit angry at me."

"A little bit." Hoss laughed.

Just then, Officer Michaelson threw on his wailer and pulled over to the side. Hoss, unsure of how to respond, pulled over behind him.

The cop got out and said, "Maxa, Cruncietti says he needs to speak to you. Get in with me."

As Rudy did so, the cop said to Hoss, "You stay within the posted speed limit, hear me? I'm gonna go a bit faster."

Michaelson went fast, very fast, and said, "Here's the deal, Maxa. We're going to the football game. Your quarterback hurt his hand and says he can't play.

His backup, some kid named Calverts, is goofing up in every possible way. Your team is dangerously close to losing this game, so guess who's gonna suit up and save the day for Claymore High?"

"Did Coach Hartman call you? How did he know where I was?"

The cop shrugged. "Claymore's a small town, Maxa. People know each other, and everyone there knows me, for obvious reasons, and I know just about everyone, too."

"I thought you were going to throw me in jail. Now you're taking me to play football."

"My job is to serve and protect the community. 'Serve and protect' can mean a hundred things, and right now I'm looking after things, and taking care of business, by delivering you to the field so you can save that game. If your team wins this one, you will save the community a lot of grief." He checked the time. "We'll be there in about six minutes."

Rudy thought it unlikely they would get there so soon, seeing that they were still on the highway. Nonetheless, the cop had his flashing lights on and all the other cars pulled off to the side. Very soon they entered the outskirts of Claymore that Rudy had come to know well. The car zoomed into downtown. Other cars honked at each other. Mitch woke up and pulled himself upright.

"Where am I?" he asked, rubbing at his eyes.

Rudy looked left and right. He saw Burned Out Park. Home sweet home. He felt unfazed by the huge challenge that awaited him. He really felt nothing at all.

"Hoss?" asked Mitch.

"Wassup, big guy?"

Mitch pointed to a man on the sidewalk. "There's Doofus. Let's go spray-paint his store."

"Another day, Mitch."

"Hold it," said Michaelson. "Is *he* the person you've been covering for?"

"Yep."

The cop opened his mouth, as if about to say something, then closed it. Finally he said, "We'll talk about this later."

Mitch leaned forward and muttered to Rudy, "What's the deal with that guy? Must be that time of the month, huh?"

Rudy suppressed a laugh. "Sit back, Mitch. We're just about there."

"Where we goin'?"

"To a football game."

"Oh. I like football," Mitch said.

CHAPTER 27

The stands at Claymore High's field were full of glum, quiet people, and the scoreboard showed numbers that those fans had not seen in a very long time. Alvin Calvert, the second-string quarterback, had thrown more interceptions than completions, and the Pioneers' only score was a field goal. Plenty of time remained on the clock, but by now they were in the fourth quarter, and a handful of fans were preparing to depart as the sound of an approaching police car broke the evening's stillness.

Some spectators paid attention when the police cruiser stopped and its passenger door swung open. When Rudy Maxa half-fell out of the vehicle, those who recognized him—and knew why he had arrived— pulled off his clothes as if he were an actor submitting to a thirty-second wardrobe change. Someone dashed away to get Rudy's football gear, and within a couple of minutes he stood there, ready for snaps. Several people carried him over to the field and released him in front of Coach Hartman.

"Ready to go, Coach," he said.

"Get in there!"

Rudy advanced a couple of steps before Mario Cruncietti jumped in his way. "Where's my father?"

"Nice to see you, too."

"Answer my question."

"He's in the cop car. On his way home. Now I gotta go play football."

"Yeah, you do that." Mario's voice was quiet and cold. "I'll deal with you afterwards."

Rudy's eyes narrowed. "You threatenin' me?"

Mario shook his head. "Not threatening—promising." He stepped aside.

In the huddle, Joe Rossi said, "Welcome to our nightmare, Rudy. Glad you could make it."

"Well, I'm here now. So let's get busy and win this thing."

He got off to an inauspicious start. He fumbled the snap, but it somehow bounced back into his hands; trouble was, he failed to get a firm grip on it, so he took a knee before the Titans could sack him. Second down was a poorly thrown pass that the cornerback nearly intercepted.

Now, at third and twelve, he decided to go back to what had always worked. He faked a passing play, slammed the ball into Joe Rossi's midsection and threw his shoulder into the first Titan who charged at them. Rossi got the hole he needed and scampered off for a sixty-two-yard gain.

A couple of plays later, Rudy had sufficiently confused his opponents that when he called the snap, the Titans didn't know which Pioneer to cover. They mostly just stood there as Rudy, on a quarterback sneak, darted past them and into the end zone.

The fans went berserk, and even Coach Hartman jumped up and down, pumping his fist into the air. Rudy, too, got so excited that his hands trembled as he held the ball for the point-after attempt, but the kicker booted it through. Suddenly, the Pioneers made a game of it, trailing 14-10.

Rudy trotted back to the sideline, and Coach Hartman gave him a hug. Then he said, "Maxa, you're not running my plays."

"My bad. I'll do better on our next possession."

Hartman frowned, as if disbelieving Rudy, but said nothing. The coach apparently thought it best not to fix things that weren't broken.

Rudy started towards the field to play cornerback. As he did so, Lauren grabbed him and said, "I know you can win this thing for us, Rudy!"

He looked in the direction of Mario on the bench. "What's the deal with him?"

She shook her head. "Don't really know. He's freaking me out a little bit."

The referee blew his whistle, and Rudy headed out to play.

Rudy and the Pioneers ruined four consecutive plays for the Titans, so Claymore High regained possession of the ball. Their quarterback received the snap and did things his own, highly unorthodox way: Handing off the football to a teammate and using Mitch's "hit 'em high, hit 'em low, just make sure you hit 'em" strategy. It paid off; the Pioneers gained five or six yards per carry, and just as the Titans got ready for the Pioneers' ground attack, Rudy stepped back and threw long to Alvin Calverts, who stood alone in the end zone.

The Pioneers' defense came in, eager to protect their small lead for the few remaining minutes of the game. Rudy, as cornerback, wished someone would turn the game clock to 00:00.

The Titans huddled, then hurried to the line of scrimmage. Rudy thought they looked like the most panicked football players he had ever seen. Their quarterback took the snap, scrambled around to evade Pioneers, then tried to force ten- and fifteen-yard passes that ended up hitting the backs of the intended receivers. On fourth and ten, they did a Hail Mary. The huge pass might have worked except that a Pioneer got a couple of fingers on it just as it left the quarterback's hand, and the ball twirled through the air in a sloppy spiral, destined for no one in particular.

Rudy, one of the fastest guys on the field, tried to get to it first. He dived for the ball, scarcely aware of anything but the ball—its texture, its brown roundness, his hands upon it—and he neither saw nor heard the big Titan who plowed into him. He was aware of something, then nothing.

Crunch!

Lights out.

CHAPTER 28

He felt a kiss on his lips. He liked it. He wanted more, lots more. He wondered if he was dreaming. His dreams had included kissing the girls. Other stuff, too.

He opened his eyes just in time to see Mario pull Lauren off him. "Enough of that," Mario said.

"Just trying to bring him around," she retorted.

Rudy sat up.

"Take it easy, Maxa," said Coach Hartman. "You'll live."

"I don't remember what happened," Rudy said.

"You took one for the team," Hartman told him.

"It's all over? We won?"

Hartman grinned. "Not exactly. Still got time on the clock. We have the ball."

"You're just waiting for me, then." Rudy got up and put on his helmet. He felt dizzy, sick to his stomach. He thought he might vomit in front of everyone. His ears rang, too. He had heard about that—tinnitus.

"You all right?" Hartman asked him.

"Rad," he replied.

Some of them looked at Lauren, as if seeking her expert opinion.

"It's football," she told them. "You can't bench

every guy who gets knocked on his butt. Pretty soon there would be no one left to play."

Hartman said, "Maxa, this one's almost a done deal. Just get out there and take a knee. Don't do any blocking. Hear me?"

"Negative," said someone behind them.

Mario.

"Shut up and sit down, Cruncietti," said Hartman.

"You got hit," Mario said to Rudy. "I'll go in for the rest of the game. I can handle the snaps and take a knee."

"What about your busted hand?" Hartman asked.

"I think I can handle snaps and take a knee."

Rudy shook his head. "This one belongs to me. I'll put it to bed."

"Bad idea. You don't want to end up like you-know-who."

"What *are* you talking about?" Hartman asked.

Rudy thought for a moment. "I'm done. You finish it, Crunch."

"Well, *somebody* better go out there!" Hartman shouted.

Mario put on his helmet and jogged onto the field.

CHAPTER 29

Mario Cruncietti ran a half-dozen plays for a few dozen yards and a couple of first downs. His performance was one of the most mediocre of his distinguished high school career, but he managed to run the clock down to zero and win the game.

At the end of the contest, Mario retired from football.

When the team met for practice on Monday, Mario was a no-show. Coach Hartman stood before his crestfallen football boys and said, "Cruncietti is gone; Maxa is our new quarterback."

"What's the reason Mario's gone?" asked Joe Rossi.

"Gee, Rossi," replied Hartman, "I don't see that that's any of your business. Let me try that again: 'Cruncietti is gone; Maxa is in.' Which part of that did you fail to understand?"

Rudy's mother said, "I'm not so sure that playing football is such a great idea. It's just so dangerous."

"There's danger everywhere in life."

"I think it's pretty clear that you got the starting job for the Pioneers because Mario Cruncietti got so freaked about his father's head injuries that he said, 'I can't do this. I've seen what happened to my old man.'"

"Ma, we don't know what Mario was thinking when he insisted on finishing the game for me. We can't hear people's thoughts—and if we could, I don't think his thoughts would be the ones we would care to hear."

"He was afraid of concussions and Alzheimer's," she said. "That's why he gave up football. Everyone says he was the best quarterback ever."

Ouch, Rudy thought. *Just ouch.*

"Maybe he *wasn't* 'the best quarterback ever,' Ma, because fear got the best of him and he lost his edge…" He said nothing more because he knew that Virginia Maxa thought everyone who played football was a little screwy in the head to begin with. He added, "I promise I'll be careful out there. If I know I've had enough, I'll sit on the bench and let someone else take over."

He knew his mother felt better about things after Officer Bruce Michaelson revealed to her that Mitch Cruncietti had been Rudy's accomplice. She then repeated the news to everyone she knew.

"Gee, Ma, why don't you just put Mitch's private business on every billboard in the Inland Valley?"

"Well, I needed to make it known that you were not a juvenile delinquent," she said. "I had to tell your father, too, so he wouldn't try to have the court declare me an unfit parent."

Rudy nodded. "OK, but only Boss Daddy. His lawyer, too."

"Plus my boss at the *Transcript*. He sees the police blotter, you know. I'm *so* happy that you're no longer in trouble. Bruce says—"

"Who's Bruce?"

"Officer Michaelson. He says that he knows you were just covering for Mitch, and that changes everything."

"I see." *Bruce?*

Rudy didn't know what to think when, a day or so later, he got home and found Officer Michaelson sitting at the Maxas' kitchen table, slurping down a glass of iced tea.

"Glad you're home, Rudy," said his mother. "Tell him the good news, Bruce."

"All charges are dropped, Rudy. No court date, no lawyers, no nothing." He smiled. "I hope that makes your day."

Rudy nodded, grateful that he would not be penalized for Mitch's stunt against Elmer the Exterminator. But why couldn't the cop simply have called them with this happy news? To Rudy, the only thing worse than being busted by a cop was watching one cruising his mom.

He shouldn't have been so surprised, though. Back in Indy a summer or two ago, when Rudy and his pals were getting old enough to notice females, Virginia Maxa, like everyone else, stripped down to her swimsuit when the Midwestern heat set in. "Hey, Rudy," his friends said, "your mom has a real cute bod. Cute *everything*." He had always suspected that Boss Daddy had married her mostly because she looked good on his arm whenever he wanted to show off for his clients, so now that she was single again, it only made sense that she would find a new partner. He supposed he should be happy for her.

"Just don't tell your boss at the *Transcript* about Mitch's medical condition," Rudy said. "Your boss can think I'm a serial killer; I don't give a crap. But I won't be having him tell the whole Inland Valley that its most famous resident has Alzheimer's."

He believed that was the least he could do for Mitch.

He now viewed Burned Out Park as if it were completely new to him. How much his life had changed since his first lonely visits to the park! He could remember kicking the ball and throwing it through the hoop all by himself, when along came Mitch, full of football lessons to teach him. Rudy stared at the bushes even now, half-expecting a surprise visit from Captain Crunch.

He looked up at the Bronze Horse, too, thinking that his buddy might be hanging out there. But no. Mitch's family, considering all that had happened, would probably never let him walk around alone again, lest the poor guy meet up with someone like Rudy Maxa.

He climbed onto the horse, believing that Mitch would want him to do so. He looked out and saw the rest of the park from nearly thirty feet above the ground, and he guessed that the fine view was what had appealed to Mitch. Rudy sat back and looked up and around for close to an hour until a harsh, cold wind started and he had to get down.

Back in his VW, he drove along the town's main drag until Elmer the Exterminator flagged him down.

"I spoke to Officer Michaelson," said the old coot. "He, uh, explained to me about how things were."

Rudy nodded, but told himself that if Elmer said

one unkind word about Mitch, he would get out of his car and knock the skinny dude on his butt.

Elmer, however, did not wish to fight. He handed Rudy a picture of his store before it was his.

"I had it in my store. I didn't know anything about it until Officer Michaelson came by and talked to me about Mister Cruncietti and what-all.

"It's an old picture of my store—only then it was called Dufus Hardware. Notice you don't see the big bug hangin' from the sign. Anyway, the old fella, Dufus, he looked a lot like me, or I look a lot like him." He chuckled.

"So in this picture you can see a couple of little brats standing outside the store. That's Mister Cruncietti and his pal. Even in that picture, you could tell they were up to something."

Rudy saw right away that the other brat was Hoss.

"I thought," Elmer said with a small, shy smile, "that you could think of someone to give this to."

"Yeah," Rudy said, "I think I can do that."

Rudy stood at the Cruncettis' front door, too embarrassed to knock on the door and say, "Hey! I brought you this. I thought you might like it."

He considered turning around and leaving when the door opened and Kimberley appeared.

"What?" she asked.

"It's me."

"So I see."

"Your bro around?"

"Negative."

"Where is he?"

Kimberley shrugged. "Search me, man."

Rudy said, "Hmm. Well, I better jam. I just came by to give you something."

He handed her the photo.

She frowned. "Uh, you gonna tell me what this is?"

"It's a framed photograph."

"Well, duh." Then, "I'm wanting this because…"

"Your dad is in it. He's one of the little kids. The other one is Hoss."

"My mom should maybe have a look at this."

"How's your day, by the way?"

Kimberley thrust out her chin a bit. "I don't really know. He's usually much worse than I think he is. Sometimes it seems like he gets worse by the minute."

"I guess I didn't help much when I took him out to Inland Valley College," Rudy said.

"Oh, you did him a big favor. You did the right thing. Even Mom and Mario think so."

"I feel real bad for him. I really do."

"I know you do." She added, "How'd you like to do him another favor?"

"Like what?"

"We need some more help with him, and my mom says he relates better to you than anyone else. We'll understand if you don't want to."

The Inland Valley Seniors Chateau did its best to look unlike the old folks' home it was. A big fine old manor house, its lobby was as magnificent as that of any celebrated resort, and it smelled of fresh flowers and furniture polish. But within a few minutes, Rudy clued into the smells of sick people and death.

"Thanks for doing this," Virginia Cruncietti said to Rudy. "He's always glad to see you, even if he thinks you're Hoss from way back when."

"Glad to help." In truth, he would have traded his VW to be at Burned Out Park rather than this house of death and sickness. But he believed he owed the Cruncietti this favor, and he took favors—giving and getting them—very seriously.

"I've never seen so many old buggers in my life," Mitch said.

Rudy wanted to laugh at the wisecrack, but the truth behind it saddened him. Mitch was right—the place *was* full of old people; the youngest of them had a couple of decades on him. A few appeared to be pushing a hundred. Not all of them were dying, or even seriously ill; some had just gotten so old that they needed more help than their families could, or wanted to, provide. Rudy felt disturbed at the notion that a big, strong, athletic man like Mitch Cruncietti was rotting away in here.

"This sucks," Mario whispered to the others. "Let's bail."

Missus Palladino, the social worker who'd accompanied them, smiled and said, "I know this may be an upsetting experience for you—"

"My father isn't ready for this," Mario said. "He shouldn't be here."

"Oh, but he *should* be here. This is the residence that's best for people with his particular medical condition. Your father has experienced an early onset of his disability, which is why he is so much younger than the other people here who have the same needs that he does."

All of them, including Mitch, moseyed down the

hallway to a puny lounge in which a few old women sat in wheelchairs and stared at a big-screen TV whose picture was scrambled.

Mitch walked over, picked up the remote and switched to a game show with an unscrambled image. "That's more like it, huh?"

The women just kept staring. Rudy wondered if they were catatonic. Rudy plopped into one of the vacant chairs and chuckled a couple of times at the insipid TV host.

"See?" said the social worker. "It's a nice fit. He can even help the others who can't help themselves."

Mitch jumped out of his seat and wheeled around to face Missus Palladino. "You talkin' about *me*? *I'm* not movin' into this joint!"

His wife stepped forward and grasped his hands with hers. "Mitch, you need to understand—"

"Do you think I'm retarded?" His lips were thin with anger, his face taut. "You think I don't know what this place is? It's for people who crap their pants and can't remember their own names. Well, I'm not gettin' any younger, but I'm not brain-dead just yet, so don't try to lock me up in here with these people." He swallowed hard and looked from his wife to his son to his daughter and finally to Rudy. "Right, Hoss?" Mitch had a catch in his voice that made him seem childlike and vulnerable.

Rudy had no idea of what to say to his friend. This was the first time Mitch had ever called him Hoss outside of Burned Out Park or one of their misadventures. On those occasions, Rudy could simply reply, "Yeah, sure, Mitch—whatever you say." But this, of course, was different; he couldn't side with Mitch when he and the Cruncietti family know that this facility was where the big man needed to be.

Rudy looked to Virginia Cruncietti for some sort of support or empathy for the confused young man, but in her face he saw only a woman struggling with her own woe.

"Mitch," he said, "I'm not Hoss. My name is Rudy Maxa."

The big man burst into tears. His wife released his hands and dug into her purse. She pulled out a handkerchief and mopped up her husband's tears. Kimberley's lips quivered; Mario swung away from them and stared out the window. Rudy closed his eyes, unable to bear the sight of Mitch being tended to by his missus.

Rudy

CHAPTER 30

Looking up at the early December sky, Rudy had to admit that California often was a nice place in which to live. Back in Indy, the cold, snowy weather would have set in by now; here in Claymore, he counted four clouds and the temperature was about fifty—just about perfect for football.

The Claymore High faithful had turned out to fill the stands and make noise for their Pioneers, who were one game away from two perfect seasons. The Pioneers, led by star quarterback Rudy Maxa, were already up by two touchdowns against the winless Hamber Heroes.

Rudy's next play was his usual thing—a handoff to Rossi, then a stiff block to create a hole for Rossi. Fifteen-yard gain. Coach Hartman freaked out a little bit each time his quarterback ran that play, and Rudy loved it.

He smiled at the sound of the roaring crowd, of the bevy of cheerleaders calling out "Roooody!" He knew this would always be Mario's team, but the guys—and the community—had made it clear that Claymore was big enough for both of them. Mario had shed his jersey and helmet to root for his team alongside his father a few rows up in the stands. Virginia stopped attending games once her son called it quits, and Kimberley stayed home to watch TV and cruise the Internet. But Mitch still wanted to go see the Pioneers, so Mario took him. Rudy imagined how much it must have irked Super Mario to watch his rival taking care of business. Rudy still thought that Mario was a dweeb, but there he was, in the stands with his dad, cheering for the Pioneers. That took some character and maturity.

Rudy called an audible but zoned out for the briefest instant and let the ball slip through his fingers. He fell on it and the referee blew the play dead.

"Come on, Maxa! School's out! Wake up!" Hartman yelled from the sideline.

That visit to the Inland Valley retirement home was a month old, but images of it kept popping up on the screen behind Rudy's eyeballs whenever he wasn't concentrating hard enough on anything else. He guessed it was doubly hard on Mitch's family. As for Mitch himself, Rudy thought it likely that the poor dude had already forgotten that visit and the presence of his name on their waiting list for future vacancies. He seemed different since that day; Kimberley said he had become listless and uninterested in life. While such a slowdown was perhaps a part of the natural aging process, it was hugely uncharacteristic of Mitch Cruncietti, the world's biggest, oldest naughty little boy.

"When we went to that seniors' center that day? It's like the place aged him by two decades," Kimberley said. "When he got up from that chair and said, 'You're not putting *me* in here!' he seemed to

196

figure out just how weak and compromised he was."
She shook her head. "It's just too sad."

Rudy gave his coach the thumbs up, to indicate
that he'd gotten his head together and was ready to
play some more football. He was pleased to see the
imminence of halftime on the scoreboard. Soon the
Pioneers would celebrate their second consecutive
undefeated season, and he would receive the high
fives and helmet pats that really belonged to Mario.

The quarterback threw his shoulder into a big
Hamber lineman and brought him low so that Rossi
could jump over him and rush to the twenty-yard line.
Another Pioneers touchdown would effectively end
the game. The bleachers practically groaned under the
bouncing bodies of fans cheering and screaming for
Rudy and his teammates to make this one a done deal.

Hartman must have wanted the same thing,
because he called for a touchdown pass for the next
play.

Rudy bluffed a handoff to Rossi, kept the ball
and moved to the right. Alvin Calverts, the intended
receiver, easily outran his defender and headed for the
end zone The pass had to hit Calverts just at the right
moment. Difficult, but hardly impossible.

He got ready to throw, looked this way and
that—and did nothing. Through his peripheral vision
he saw a tall, broad man climbing the stadium stairs.
Could that be *Mitch*? Then he spotted Mario seated
where Mitch had been, and the former quarterback
watched Rudy.

*He's probably thinking, 'I could make that play, sucker.
Let's see you do it!'*

*Mario, do you know that your father has wandered off?
Do you care?*

As the other Pioneers screamed at him to throw the ball, Rudy tucked it in and eluded an approaching Hero. He looked again up into the stands and noticed why Mitch was climbing the stairs. For what?

Then Rudy saw the falcon on top of the wall.

He remembered what Michael Hossman had said about Fanny's departure and Hoss's expectation that on some day the big bird would return.

Could Mitch be flashing back on that? Could he believe that the falcon sitting there was Fanny from that day a zillion years ago…?

Rudy yelled "Mitch!" as he dashed to the sideline and dropped the ball at Hartman's feet. The coach scowled and yelled, but Rudy just kept on towards the stairs.

Mitch had nearly climbed the wall when the crowd figured out what Rudy was doing. The big, agile man, just a few feet from the falcon, got to his feet on top of the concrete wall and stood still for a moment, as if to get his bearings.

Rudy hollered through burning lungs, *"Stop! Don't!"*

Mitch stood stock still and fixed Rudy with a clear-eyed, clear-headed stare that the young man remembered seeing at Inland Valley College as Mitch spoke from the stage.

Then Mitch took a big step towards the falcon, and Rudy covered his eyes with his hands. When he looked again, the bird and man were gone.

CHAPTER 31

Rudy put on his only suit to go to his first funeral since childhood. His great grandmother, known to all as "Gram," had died at one hundred one. Her funeral in Indiana, attended by maybe two dozen people, had bored Rudy senseless.

"Where are the others?" he had asked his mother.

"In the graveyard. She outlived most of her friends and admirers."

"When *I* die, I hope I have zillions of friends and admirers at my funeral."

"Why? You won't be there to enjoy it."

Mitch Cruncietti, due to his relatively early death at fifty-three and the fact that most of the people his age were still alive, had a standing-room-only funeral on a rainy, windy morning. By the time Rudy and his mother arrived, they had to huddle under umbrellas and listen to the eulogies through the public-address system. The rain and cold made Rudy uncomfortable, and wearing his Sunday best wasn't much fun, either, but the weather and his apparel were trivial matters to him. He realized that he had funerals—he hated *death*, especially when it happened to those who meant something to him—and he hoped he wouldn't have to dress up again and say goodbye to another friend or relative for a long, long time.

Most of Claymore seemed to have shown up to say goodbye to Mitch. Rudy guessed that these folks had already forgiven the dead man for compromising the Pioneers' back-to-back perfect seasons. Maybe the townspeople had decided that there were more important things than high school football.

As he adjusted his umbrella to keep himself and his mom as dry as possible, Rudy concluded that Mitch's family had done a fine job of keeping his illness their secret. Captain Crunch had gotten plenty of attention as Claymore's hero, but Rudy alone had figured out that the man had Alzheimer's. Mitch's behavior had mostly just enhanced his image—people called him "eccentric," "colorful," "quite the character"—and didn't every community like its heroes and celebrities to be such oddballs?

His final moments with Mitch disturbed Rudy: He saw Mitch going for the falcon; he stopped looking; he resumed looking and saw no Mitch. He knew that fallen, or jumped, and what was left of him was now a sauce upon the pavement. He supposed that if he had been Mitch, he would have wanted to go out the same way.

Mitch's death went reasonably well reported online. Some NFL retirees, now looking like bears in thousand-dollar suits, went to the funeral and sat inside the chapel while Rudy and his mom stood outside in the rain. He didn't mind; he felt glad that those guys, who surely had better things to do, came all the way out to Claymore to say goodbye to Mitch.

Following the service, most of the mourners went away. Only those closest to the deceased and his family went to the Crunciettis' home to comfort the family. *Bereaved but relieved*, Rudy said to himself.

"You don't have to go in there," Kathleen Maxa said to her son.

"You're right—I don't have to. I don't *want* to, either. But I'm going in anyway."

She pinched his cheek. "You're a terrific kid. Please forgive me if I ragged on you about things."

"You're forgiven." Then, "How's Officer Bruce these days?"

She frowned. "What's that supposed to mean?"

"Hey, I have no beefs with him. You sure don't, either."

"Yes, I like him a lot. Is that a problem?"

"Negative. You're entitled to some happiness, I guess."

"Affirmative."

Rudy got out of the car and promised to call his mom when he was ready to leave. She drove off and he went into the Crunciettis' house, expecting a quiet, dark, sad place with people crying. Instead, it looked like the busiest restaurant in town, with orders shouted into the kitchen and plates of food and glasses of beer and wine brought out.

Much of the conversation, of course, was about Mitch—fond anecdotes about what he had said and done—but they talked about other things, too, like how America's first non-white president was doing and if Hillary Clinton would ever make it into the White House.

Rudy noticed Mario standing off to the side with a handful of Pioneers, all of them wearing white shirts and black ties under their varsity jackets. Lauren clung to Mario, and Rudy wondered what was up with *that*.

He watched them exit the funeral that way, but considering that this had been one of the saddest days of Mario life, maybe Lauren was just trying to be supportive. But no; if Mario and Lauren had been an on-again, off-again item, you didn't have to be a genius to figure out what their relationship status was now. Lauren looked much too gorgeous in her black dress, as if she already a member of the Cruncietti family. Rudy watched as Kimberley, sitting by her mother, flashed an evil eye at Lauren.

Rudy looked at Lauren and Mario for a moment or two, but when she made eye contact with him, he looked at the food-laden table at his side. Picking up a tuna salad sandwich, he stuffed it into his mouth and closed his eyes, just then realizing how hungry he was.

He felt a tug on his sleeve and opened his eyes to see Lauren standing before him.

"Hey," she said.

"Hey," he said back.

"I want to explain something. I'm sure you saw me with Mario just now."

He nodded.

"Mario needs me now, during this difficult time." She spoke in a quiet voice; he had to read her full pink lips. "I suppose he's needed me all along, but he didn't want me to see what was happening to his dad."

He nodded again. Mitch had just died, and here was Lauren, in her mourning attire, at his son's side. To Rudy, it looked as if Mario wasn't kidding around with Lauren or chasing other girls. He was ready to make a commitment to her.

"You and Mario," he said, nodding. "You look good together. Even when you and I started hanging out, your mind was mostly on him."

She smiled and blushed. "I guess it looked that way to you. But the truth is, when you and I spent time together, I liked it. I liked *you*."

He shrugged. "We had fun."

She nodded and wandered back over to Mario and the Pioneers. By then, the rain had stopped and the clouds drifted apart. Some of the NFL guys gathered in the back yard, heehawing about Captain Crunch and how he'd creamed them.

"He hit me so hard once that I forgot where and who I was…"

"Mitch drilled me that my ears rang for a dozen days. Last time my ears rang like that was after a Van Halen concert."

"He banged me up so much that I was afraid I was gonna die and I was afraid I was gonna survive…"

Michael Hossman told them about Rudy's drive out to Yardbird to enlist his aid in getting Mitch out to Inland Valley College. Then he said, "It's such a blessing that Mitch had a friend like you towards the end of his life."

"I'm not sure I had any business acting against his family's wishes." Rudy then felt uncomfortable and excused himself. He wanted to get out of there and go home.

Inside the house, Rudy said goodbye to Kimberley and she hugged him. "You were so kind to my dad. You were really great to him."

"I gotta split," he muttered.

"Thanks for everything. Catch you at school."

"Uh huh."

He decided not to call his mother. Now that the weather had improved, he would walk home, even though his house was over a mile away. No problem; he needed to walk and sort out some things in his head. Mitch's death had seemed so overwhelming and tragic that Rudy kept forgetting that his friend had been only one of seven billion people walking the planet, and the world would continue without him. Rudy, too, would continue this business of life, and soon Mitch Cruncietti would fade into just another trivial image in a young man's mind. Rudy resolved to become a better son to his mother, and maybe even go on some of her photography trips and learn about online journalism.

On his way down the hall towards the Crunciettis' front door, he saw an open doorway and looked in. There he saw Mario watching TV. Mario looked up and waved him inside.

"Sorry about your dad," he said, wondering if Mario would throw a punch at him.

Mario pointed at the TV. "Check it out."

"What is it?"

"Raiders versus Bears. Way back when."

Rudy sat and watched. Walter Payton took a handoff and was plowed by a Raider. "Payton loses five on that one!" shouted the announcer. "Nobody fooled Mitch Cruncietti on that play! Anyone wonder why they call him Captain Crunch?"

"Wow!" Rudy shook his head. "I never actually saw him play."

"'Wow!' is right. I watch this footage and see him using his head like a pile driver. Who told him that was OK? Why didn't anyone warn him? He must've had hundreds of little head injuries that added up to one big, life-destroying concussion. And he didn't even know it."

A few moments later, Rudy said, "I want to thank you for being such a good sport about sitting on the bench while I played for the Pioneers."

"I want to thank *you* for taking my dad out to his hall of fame ceremony."

The two guys shook hands, and Rudy walked home. On his way, he passed by Burned Out Park. He went in, climbed onto the Bronze Horse, and stared into the sky, thinking of Mitch Cruncietti and a zillion other things.